NANCY WARREN

CHAPTER AND CURSE

VAMPIRE BOOK CLUB
BOOK TWO

Cover Design by Lou Harper of Cover Affairs

ISBN: ebook 978-1-928145-84-4

ISBN: print 978-1-928145-83-7

Ambleside Publishing

INTRODUCTION

A quiet Irish village? Not so much!

An ancient curse seems to be causing bad luck in the charming village of Ballydehag, Ireland—witch Quinn Callahan's new home. When someone is murdered is it the curse? Or is there a very human murderer on the loose? Moving to a small Irish village was supposed to keep the middle-aged witch out of trouble. Yeah, that didn't happen. Quinn and her bookish vampires must find the real killer and end the curse before someone else dies.

If you like quirky characters, mystery, humor and a touch of romance, don't miss this second installment in the *Vampire Book Club* series from the best-selling author of *The Vampire Knitting Club*. Each book is a complete story that can be read on its own.

If you haven't met Rafe Crosyer yet, he's the gorgeous, sexy vampire in *The Vampire Knitting Club* series. You can get his origin story free when you join Nancy's no-spam newsletter at NancyWarrenAuthor.com.

Come join Nancy in her private Facebook group where we talk about books, knitting, pets and life. www.facebook.com/groups/NancyWarrenKnitwits

CHAPTER AND CURSE

CHAPTER 1

"*A*re you not ready?" Kathleen McGinnis asked me as she came into my bookshop.

I glanced up from unpacking a new order of books in The Blarney Tome in Ballydehag, Ireland. "Ready for what?"

Kathleen McGinnis, the local grocer and my sister witch, was more dressed up than usual, wearing a flowered dress with a pale blue cardigan. She'd also curled her hair and sported fresh lipstick. She clucked her tongue against the roof of her mouth. "Billy O'Donnell's wake, of course."

"Why would I go to Billy O'Donnell's wake? I barely knew the man."

"He was a customer here for years."

"But I've been here for less than a month." I thought Billy O'Donnell had bought some books on Roman history and was a train-spotter, but that could have been Billy O'Connell. In fact, I wasn't completely sure which one of them was dead.

She came toward me. "It's a mark of respect. Everyone in Ballydehag will be there. Besides, it's a chance for you to mingle with the locals. Get them to know and trust you."

After I'd exposed a murderer and a few dark secrets of this small town along the way, I felt the townspeople looking at me askance, like they were pleased to have a murderer caught but not sure about the collateral damage. Kathleen was right. The more time I spent socializing with my new neighbors, the sooner they'd lower their guard around me. At least I hoped so. "But who will look after my shop?"

She shook her head at me. "There won't be any business. Everybody in town will be at Billy O'Donnell's."

I looked down at my jeans and blue silk shirt. "Can I go home and change?"

"No, no. There's no time. Here, this'll do."

She dashed to where I had a sweater hanging on a hook. It was black and hip-length and had been hanging there for a couple of weeks. I didn't want to wear it though, as it was a warm June day. I'd be sweltering. Still, I did as I was told and put the sweater on. She stood back and nodded. "It's a shame about the jeans. Never mind. Everyone knows you're an American."

Then, I am not kidding, she pulled a pink plastic comb from out of her capacious handbag and tidied up my hair. As though she were my grandmother. I waited for her to spit on her hankie and wipe my face, but luckily she didn't go that far. Then she stood back, looking quite pleased with herself. "There. That'll do. Now come along. We don't want to be late."

I really doubted Billy O'Donnell would notice if we were late or not.

We left the bookshop, and I locked the door behind me. Kathleen had parked her grocery van out front, and so I climbed in the passenger seat, and we set off. Every shop on the high street was shut, and it looked as though every soul who called Ballydehag home was heading for the wake. I didn't really mind being hustled off to pay my respects to a man I'd barely known. In fact, I was quite excited to go. I'd never been to a wake before.

I soon noticed a wonderful scent coming from the back of the van. "What smells so good?"

"I've a tray of ham sandwiches and champ and brack."

"Champ and Brack? What are they? A pair of wrestlers?"

She made a sound, half amusement and half irritation. Cerridwen made the same noise when I rescued a mouse she had her eye on.

"Champ is a cooked potato dish, potatoes baked with butter and cream and leeks. And brack is an Irish fruit bread."

"Sounds like a whole van of comfort food." And I couldn't wait to tuck in.

"Well, when do you more need comfort than when you've lost someone dear to you?"

"What happened to Billy O'Connell?"

"O'Donnell!"

"Right. That one." Roman history. Trains.

"He suffered a heart attack and died at home." She shook her head. "He said he was eighty years old and if it was his time, he'd thank the good lord to take him from his own bed. Absolutely refused to go to hospital. Dr. Milsom was ever so good. He managed to keep him alive until Brenda could arrive. Brenda's his daughter. Drove all the way from Dublin, she did. It was touch and go, though. She barely made it in time. Father O'Flanagan had already administered last rites. But at least she was there to say goodbye before her father passed. I hear he roused enough to speak a few words to her."

"That's nice." What else could I say? I tried to recall what he'd looked like, and my memories were vague. I thought he'd been a tall, gaunt, bald man. He'd come into my shop looking for a book on Roman history and left with one about trains. It was hard to get too emotionally invested in the death of a man I wasn't sure I remembered.

Since she knew Ballydehag better than I did, I assumed she was correct in the proper etiquette in a situation like this. I felt I was pushing myself into a grief that I had no part in, but she said it was simply a mark of respect to go to the man's home and pay my respects to his daughter.

"He didn't have a wife?"

"No. He's been widowed some years now. They just had the one child, Brenda. But she lives in Dublin now. She's a solicitor. Very clever woman."

We drove past the church where a large orange banner hung across the main entrance, one I hadn't seen before. It was very eye-catching against the gray stone. "Save our Steeple" it said, in big white letters, and then in slightly smaller ones underneath, "Donate Generously to our Building Fund."

"Is the church falling down?" I asked as we headed down a leafy road with some of the nicest houses I'd seen in Ballydehag.

"Not falling down, no. But the new priest, Father O'Flanagan, says the steeple's unsound and he wants to smarten up the old graveyard. It's an expensive project."

I could imagine. "I didn't know Father O'Flanagan was new here. Like me."

"He's been here going on five years, now."

"Five years and he's still the new priest? When will I be considered settled then?"

She glanced at me with a twinkle in her eyes, and I suspected the answer to that was never.

Kathleen pulled the van over to the gravel shoulder. "Here we are," she said.

Billy O'Donnell's house had once been a grand old place. It had the lovely bones of a substantial residence, but the home had seen better days. I was no expert, but I thought it was Georgian, with six evenly spaced windows on the upper level and a matching set of windows below. The front garden was overgrown with weeds, and the front door needed painting. There were cars lined up along the street, and ahead of us an older couple were walking into the house.

"He lived here alone?" This was a house for a big family, with room for servants. One old man would have rattled around the empty rooms.

"He did." She opened the back of the van and picked up a box containing a large casserole dish. She gestured to me to take a second box. As we headed up the cracked path, we stepped over weeds. "Shame he let the place go. Rosaleen, his wife, would have a fit if she saw her home looking so shabby."

Kathleen didn't knock, just opened the door and walked in, and I followed. I was hit by an instant image of elegance in decay. The house appeared shabby from the outside, and the interior was no better. The red and black patterned rug must have been the height of elegance once. Long before I was born. It covered the floor. The hallway was high-ceilinged and dominated (when you got over that carpet) by a chandelier dull with dust. The walls were painted dark gold, and against the far wall, a grandfather clock loomed, grim-faced, ticking so loud I felt I must be late for something.

The old carpet showed signs of a fresh vacuuming, and an antique sideboard looked hastily cleared and wiped. I could see a thick pile of dust that had been overlooked in one corner.

Fresh flowers sat on the sideboard, heavy-scented lilies and roses and spears of greenery.

"We'll take the food through to the kitchen first," Kathleen instructed. I followed her down the corridor and into the kitchen. I could hear a murmur of voices and, oddly, a burst of laughter coming from the front room.

The kitchen was huge, with old-fashioned appliances and wood cabinets that had been new about 1970. There was patterned orange and yellow lino on the floor. An old wooden table with mismatched chairs sat against the wall. At the back of the kitchen, hooks still held outdoor coats, and there was a pair of man's boots waiting at the back door.

A group of women, wearing their Sunday best, worked with various degrees of efficiency in the kitchen. "Pass me that basket, will ye, Rosie?" a large, commanding-looking woman said, standing at the old stove as though she owned it.

Rosie Higgins, the butcher's wife, complied, and the woman opened the old oven and popped scones into the basket. "Right, those can go through to the dining room."

Rosie Higgins passed by us, carrying the basket of scones, with a quick greeting for Kathleen and a curt nod to me.

"Do ye need the oven, Kathleen?" the large woman asked, seeing us put the boxes on the countertop.

"I do not. I've brought my warmers along." And she unpacked her box, and I discovered it was a chafing dish, kept warm by a spirit lamp beneath it. The potatoes looked and smelled delicious. Like scalloped potatoes, only richer.

My box held the brack fruitbread, and it was already sliced on a pretty plate and buttered. All I had to do was take off the wrapping. Same with the ham sandwiches. I followed Kathleen into the dining room, where a buffet had been set out. There was a lot of bustling and chitchat as women leaned over each other, placing bowls and plates of goodies on a tablecloth so white and freshly ironed that it clearly hadn't come out of this house. Someone had brought it along with them, and I suspected the local ladies were also responsible for the clean plates and glasses. Either that or there'd been a lot of hasty washing up.

I placed the sandwiches and fruit bread where Kathleen told me to and looked around.

Apart from a dining table that would seat eight, there were two overcrowded glass-fronted cabinets. Dusty china, including a pretty tea set, a couple of old toy war tanks and a naval ship that looked to be made of tin, a china doll with a cracked face, and a collection of what I thought might be snuff boxes were crammed together in one. The other was filled with dull-looking crystal. Waterford, I thought. There was everything from sherry glasses to candlesticks and candy dishes. A spider made a slow tour of a brandy snifter. A heavy buffet took up a side wall, and on it were glasses that were too clean to have come from that cabinet as well as open bottles of wine.

I poured myself a glass of white wine and wandered across the hall into the living room.

I felt a buzz of discomfort, almost like an electric shock as I crossed the threshold. And immediately discovered the cause. A coffin sat in the middle of the room, on top of a table, so it was nice and high.

Inside it was Billy O'Donnnell, the center of attention. I supposed that was only fair as it was his party, but the man was dead and resting in his casket. His open casket.

Kathleen walked right up to the casket and spoke softly to its inhabitant.

I wasn't ready for that yet, so I took a look around. The place needed a good clear-out. It would be going too far to say Billy O'Donnell had been a hoarder, but there was a lot of junk in the room. Every surface was covered with dusty ornaments and bits of what looked like machinery and mechanical parts. I could see there'd been some attempt to tidy things up, and again there were marks of a quick vacuum job on the faded red carpet and a flighty duster had flirted with the dusty wood tables, but it would take a crew about a week to clean and organize the house. It was a shame, because beneath the junk and clutter, it was a lovely old home.

The original woodwork was faded and pocked but beautiful all the same. The flaking paint didn't disguise the high ceilings. The big fireplace was marble and flanked by glass-fronted bookcases crammed with books. The windows desperately needed washing, but they were lovely. At the edges where the stained and faded rug ended were beautiful hardwood floors.

Standing beside the casket was a woman about my age with a semi-frozen smile on her face as people offered her condolences. She had red-gold hair and that skin that seems particularly Irish, fine and the color of cream. I couldn't tell from here, but I suspected there was a dusting of freckles across the top of her cheeks and probably the bridge of her nose. She wore a simple black dress and pearls. She held her back carefully upright.

I let my gaze wander around the room, looking at these people who were now my neighbors, many of whom I was beginning to know. Certainly the bookish ones I knew.

Taking a steadying breath, I made my way to the casket and peeked in. I was right. Billy O'Donnell had been the one who liked Roman history and trains. He looked much better groomed now than he had in life. He wore a black suit that had probably fit him a couple of decades ago when he'd weighed more. His thin hair was neatly combed, the gaunt face shaved and his hands folded neatly over his chest.

I didn't know what to say. We hadn't been chatting acquaintances, so I settled on, "May your road be easy." That sounded vaguely like an Irish blessing as given by an American witch. Then I waited to pay my respects to the brand-new orphan. Did you call someone an orphan when they were in middle age?

People were talking in a polite, stilted way to Brenda O'Donnell, the way one does to a virtual stranger. I got the feeling that she might have grown up here, but she'd been gone for a long time, and it didn't look as though she'd kept in touch very well.

When a couple drifted away and she was standing there alone, I thought I'd whip in and pay my respects so I could get out of here. I said, "I'm so sorry for your loss." Yes, the words were trite and clichéd, but I couldn't offer her anything more personal since I didn't know her and I hadn't known her father.

"Thank you. You're very kind," she said, almost by rote, as though she'd said the same words a hundred times already.

Which I was certain she had. Her eyes looked tired, but I didn't see any sign of recent tears. She looked at me, and then her gaze sharpened slightly. "Should I know you?"

I immediately felt terrible, like she was accusing me of crashing her father's wake, which, essentially, I was doing. I rushed into speech. "I'm fairly new in town. My name is Quinn Callahan. I run the bookshop. I wouldn't have come— I barely knew your father—but I understood it's considered good manners here."

Her face softened. "It is at that. And from your voice, it sounds like you're American?"

"I am. From Seattle."

"Oh, my. I think we have some people in Seattle, but we've lost touch."

I felt that that would be the end of our conversation, and I was preparing to move away when she stopped me. "The bookshop, did you say?" She waved a hand toward the over-crowded bookcases, and an expression of bewilderment came over her face. "There is so much stuff in this house to get rid of, I don't even know where to begin. Does your bookshop accept secondhand volumes?"

She sounded so desperate, I didn't want to tell her I had to be judicious in taking secondhand books. Otherwise I'd be buried under them. I wanted to refuse, but her eyes looked heavy and sad, and my compassion kicked in. I told her I'd be happy to take her father's books. I could always donate the ones I had no use for. It must be awful to try and deal with all this junk while grieving.

I was glad I hadn't quibbled when she sighed with relief. "That's very good news. I had no idea he had so many books."

Oh, great.

I was getting ready to tell her I couldn't pay a lot for his old books. If they were anything like the junk that was in plain view, they'd be tattered old paperbacks nobody would want. But while I was trying to find a tactful way to say so, she said, "I wouldn't want any money for them. I simply want to get rid of them."

Well, that was a relief. Now my biggest worry was getting rid of the junk once she'd passed it on to me. But at least I lived here, and I had the time.

"I've got to get back to Dublin. I've a busy practice, and this is the worst week to have to take time off."

She sounded like her father dying was a real inconvenience. But I knew grief took people in different ways. Some shut down; some got very busy. Clearly Brenda O'Donnell was one of the latter types. She glanced around, and I followed her gaze. "Trash and treasure. Poor Da could never tell the difference. I know he's got some expensive things, but how am I ever going to find them underneath all this rubbish?"

I had no idea. I was just glad I wasn't the one tasked with sorting it all out. I wished her good luck and then, as a couple was coming forward to pay their respects, I slipped away. Dr. Milsom and Father O'Flanagan were standing by the window in deep discussion. Since Dr. Milsom, a cynical Englishman who'd left a busy London practice to come to this sleepy Irish village, didn't strike me as a religious zealot, I wasn't particularly surprised when I grew closer to hear them talking about fishing. I smiled and kept walking, and then a nervous-looking young guy with bright red hair said, "Excuse me, Father O'Flanagan. I'm not sure about that tree."

The old priest stopped in the middle of his fishing story and turned. "What's that?"

"I know ye asked me to cut back that yew at the edge of the graveyard, but I don't think I can."

The priest looked shocked and then suddenly annoyed. "You're not going to spout some foolish, old superstition at me, are you?"

The young man shuffled his feet and looked abashed. "It's not me, Father. It's the neighbors."

"I'm not asking you to cut down the tree. But we must prune it back. Its roots are disturbing the graves, and the branches reach out so far, they're a danger to the church during a windstorm. We're in the middle of a capital campaign to improve St. Patrick's. It's important maintenance."

"I'm sorry, Father. It gives me a bad feeling."

"I'm disappointed in you, Archie. I won't pretend otherwise."

He hung his head. "Yes, Father. Sorry, Father."

As the young man walked away, Father O'Flanagan turned back to Andrew Milsom. "The graveyard is in decay, and I've got my hands full trying to raise money to restore it and the old church tower without my own parishioners refusing to lift a finger." He shook his head. "In this day and age, wouldn't you think people would have more sense than to believe in witches and ancient curses?"

CHAPTER 2

I thought Father O'Flanagan might be quite surprised if he learned that two witches were at the wake even now. I moved out of earshot, knowing I'd be asking Kathleen what this curse was all about and how it related to a tree bordering the local graveyard.

All around me I heard the condolences and the oft-repeated phrase, "I'm so sorry about your dad."

I wondered where my own dad was sometimes. Dead, probably. He'd been unable to cope with the fact that his wife was a witch, and he'd left us when I was twelve and began to come into my power. I hadn't seen him since.

My eyes drifted back to the casket, and I was thrown back in time to my mother dying of cancer. I'd begged her to save herself, but this woman who could make the house tidy itself and light my birthday candles without the aid of a match said she couldn't. Mother had smiled and said Fate was stronger than anyone.

Sometimes I still wanted to kick Fate where it hurt, as it had done to me.

Rosie now stood beside her husband, Sean Higgins, both studiously avoiding me. I did feel guilty, though I really didn't know why I should. I had, in trying to find a man's killer, revealed that Rosie was cheating on her husband, the butcher. Neither of them had killed the man, but at the time, I hadn't known that.

Sean Higgins happened to catch my eye, and his whole face hardened before he deliberately looked away. I'd caught a murderer, but that didn't matter to him. I'd made a fool of him in a small town where he'd been an important figure. However, in reality, it wasn't me who'd made a fool of him; it was his wife. It was no consolation that I could see he treated her with the same fury and contempt he was sending my way.

Declan O'Connor, the baker, had been intimate with not only Rosie Higgins but also Karen Tate, a single woman who owned a secondhand store called Granny's Drawers.

Karen was close to my age and also single. It had seemed like we might become friends, but I'd exposed her secret affair with the baker as well—and our promising friendship had died on the vine. I sure knew how to make friends.

Would I have been better to have stayed out of it? I sometimes thought that's how some of the people in the small town of Ballydehag felt. Now that Declan O'Connor was gone, O'Connor's Bread and Buns sat shuttered and forlorn, and all our bread came pre-wrapped from Finnegan's Grocery Store.

I'd tried so hard to fit in. All my life, I'd been different. Being a witch pretty much ensures that will happen. But coming here, I'd thought I was getting a new start. Sure, my American accent made me stick out, but I'd been so hopeful that I could live a normal life. It didn't seem like that was going to happen.

To my surprise, Karen Tate came over to where I was standing. She nodded toward the open casket in the middle of the living room. "Takes some getting used to, I imagine, if it's not part of your culture."

I was so grateful to have someone appreciate how strange this was. "I've never partied with a dead guy before."

She laughed. "You'll get used to it." I did not think that was ever going to happen.

Karen looked awkward for a moment and then said, "We talked about getting together for dinner, but somehow it never happened."

There wasn't any somehow about it. After I'd exposed her affair to everyone in town, I'd not been a bit surprised that I wasn't showered with invitations from her or anyone else. If it weren't for Kathleen, the only other witch in town, and the local vampires who met weekly in my shop for their late-night book club, I wouldn't have any social life at all.

Karen continued, with false breeziness, "It's just been so busy."

She ran a secondhand store in a small village in Ireland, she was single with no children, and I didn't even think she had pets. How busy could she be? But I nodded as though we were a couple of CEOs of Fortune 500 companies. "I know. I don't know where the time goes."

"I tell you what, why don't we go to the pub for dinner? I don't know about you, but I get sick of cooking for myself."

I was delighted to have someone to go to the pub with. If she was extending an olive branch, I was grabbing onto the other end with both hands. "Absolutely. I'd love to."

She glanced over at Brenda O'Donnell, who had a glassy-eyed look, as she accepted condolences from Giles Murray, the town photographer, and his girlfriend, Beatrice. "Shall we ask Brenda to join us?"

What a goodhearted woman she was. I nodded enthusiastically. I couldn't imagine how hard it must be for Brenda. "Tonight?"

"Not tonight. It's customary to sit with the body until the funeral tomorrow."

"I didn't know that." What a horrible thing to have to do. "And she probably won't want to come out for dinner the day she buries her dad. Shall we try for the next day?"

She nodded. "I'll see what Brenda says."

When she went toward Brenda, Kate O'Leary took her place. Mrs. O'Leary was a local schoolteacher and one of my best customers. We chatted about books we were looking forward to, including the posthumous release of Bartholomew Branson's last thriller. She was dragged away by her husband, and I looked around for another friendly face.

Andrew Milsom left Father O'Flanagan. I watched him walk up to the open casket and glance in. He said a few words to the dead man, and then he went up to Brenda and they chatted for a few minutes. He went to the sideboard where the drinks were set up and poured himself a whiskey. Drink in hand, he glanced around the room and spotted me and walked over to where I was standing.

"What do you think of the Irish wake?" he asked me. Since he was English, not Irish, it must be as peculiar to him as it was to me. Though, being a doctor, he was presumably more accustomed to dead people. He was also the local coroner and pathologist.

"I find it unnerving."

He chuckled. "It is that. But the Irish don't pretend that death happens somewhere else. They embrace it. I suppose we could all learn something from that attitude."

No doubt he was right, but there had to be a happy medium.

Karen Tate came over then and greeted Andrew Milsom, and the three of us made small talk until he was hailed by an older couple who said, "Now, Andrew, you must settle an argument between us."

He excused himself and went to them. Karen said, "I don't think Brenda's up for it. Shall we just go ourselves tonight then?"

I didn't have to consult my social calendar. I knew I was free. "That sounds great. Seven?"

"I'll see you there."

"Great." We stood there for another awkward moment. I didn't know what to say, and she didn't seem to either. I hoped we made out better over dinner. Finally, she said, "I'll see if they need my help in the kitchen," and made her escape.

I'd been fighting a feeling of heaviness ever since I came into this house. No doubt it was the dead man lying in the living room and I was too sensitive. I felt the urge to get out as quickly as I could. I had made my condolences to his daughter. Surely I could go.

Kathleen McGinnis had been making the rounds of the room and now came over to me. "You've got a funny look on your face. Are you feeling all right?"

I pulled her out of the main living room and into the hallway. "I'm not big on this partying with the dead guy thing," I told her in a low voice. "Isn't it giving you a really creepy feeling?"

She seemed to think about it for a minute. "It's probably because you're not Irish. We do this all the time, Quinn. You'll have to get used to it. I don't feel any more dark than on any other sad occasion. Billy lived a good life. It was his time. The whole idea of a wake is to celebrate a life and send the soul on its way."

"Are you sure he went peacefully? Because something doesn't feel right to me."

She lowered her voice even more and said sternly, "Don't you be causing trouble, Quinn Callahan. He had a good life, and he died in his own bed with his loved ones around him. We should all be so lucky. If you're being plagued by dark thoughts, no doubt it's your own guilty conscience causing them."

I hadn't thought of that. Could she be right? The fact that I had messed with death and dragged my ex-husband back, even only for a couple of months, weighed heavy on my conscience. I shouldn't have done it, and I'd been punished. Maybe every time death was close, I would get kicked in the gut. I put a hand to my stomach. "I think I'll leave soon. I don't feel so good."

"Well, give it a few more minutes. It would look very rude if you left so quickly."

I asked her where the bathroom was. Maybe if I splashed some cold water on my face and tried to pull myself together, I could manage half an hour of being polite to people I barely knew and pretend not to notice the open coffin.

"The family bathroom's up the stairs at the end of the hall."

I walked up the stairs. The banister was beautiful. Oak or mahogany or some very nice, rich wood. It could use a good polishing, and the carpet was worn and frayed. I was no home renovator, but I felt that this lovely old home could be very grand again given half a chance. I got to the top of the stairs and went down the hall. The doors on either side were closed, bedrooms, presumably.

There was no one up here but me, as far as I knew, but I had that itchy feeling between my shoulders as though eyes were watching me. I was conscious of an urge to turn and run back down where there were other people. I had to stop it. I found the bathroom and shut myself in. It was big and old-fashioned. More dated even than the one in my cottage. The toilet had an old cistern above it, and you pulled the chain to flush. I washed my hands and glanced up into the mirror.

But it wasn't my own face I saw. A terrifying old woman stared back at me. She had scraggly gray hair, intense dark eyes and a sunken mouth. The image was wrinkled and faded like a sepia photograph, which somehow made it more scary. But while the image might be faded, the anger I felt was strong and clear as though the image had reached out and clutched my heart and was squeezing it in a scrawny claw. I gasped and jumped back and banged into the door.

I had to get out of here. I opened the door and nearly crashed into Tara, the young woman who ran the coffee shop, Cork Coffee Company. She took one look at me and put her hand on my shoulder. "Quinn, are you all right? You look like you've seen a ghost."

I laughed, hysterically and weakly. "No. Just my face reflected in the mirror. I need to get more sleep."

She nodded her head. "I know how you feel. I could use a

couple of weeks at the beach with my feet up and a good book."

I nodded.

She went in, and I waited outside the door for a scream. But it never came. Maybe she hadn't seen the scary face in the mirror. Maybe hag face had only appeared to me. Oh, lucky me.

I walked back downstairs, feeling shaken. This house was seriously haunted.

I looked for Kathleen to tell her I'd find my own way back to town. I saw her standing beside an old woman who was watching Brenda with such an expression of pride and affection that I assumed it was her mother. But it couldn't be, because her mother had died some time ago. Presumably that was why the house was such a mess, since the father had been living here all by himself before he passed away.

The woman was probably eighty, but she wasn't going gently into that dark night. She was fighting old age every inch of the way. She stood straight and tall, her white hair was styled, and while her black dress and jacket weren't new, they were stylish. The only concession I could see to her age was the flat shoes she wore. I bet she'd worn heels when she was young and hated to give up and go into the flat ones. Still, it suggested she was sensible in that she put away her vanity in favor of safety.

I managed to catch Kathleen's eye, but instead of coming my way, she beckoned me over. I knew the ghost couldn't hurt me, probably. I'd make nice for a few more minutes and then tell Kathleen my intuition was telling me to get out of here.

As I went up and said hello to the woman, she looked at me with her head to one side. "I never taught you, did I?"

Ah. Not mother but proud teacher. That made sense. Brenda would have been any teacher's pet, I imagined, given how well she'd done in life.

Kathleen said, "This is Quinn Callahan. She's only recently moved here. Quinn, this is Bridget Sullivan. She was one of my favorite teachers."

Bridget Sullivan took my hand in hers. "Quinn. Of course. You run the bookshop. I've heard all about you, and I've been meaning to come in and have a good browse. Lucinda kept the shop well stocked with a mixture of high- and lowbrow titles. I hope you do the same."

"I try to follow Lucinda's principles. Please come by. I'll wager my tea is better than hers."

"My eyes aren't what they used to be. But I do still love to read. I don't suppose you get any large-print books in?"

"I have a few. But I could always bring in something specially for you if you want me to."

I was perfectly aware that she could order anything online, or with e-readers now, she could set the font as large as she needed to. Still, bookstores like mine kept going by offering personal service. At least that was my theory. If there was a book she specially wanted, I would get it for her.

"Did you teach Brenda?" I asked her.

And that started her off nicely. "Oh, yes. I taught English, you know, and she was always a bright, intelligent girl. With such a promising future." And then her eyes clouded over. "It wasn't easy for her. But she got there in the end. Started out at Cork University and then got all the way to the School of Law in Trinity College, Dublin." She said the words as though reading them from Brenda's degree. "Oh, yes, I'm very proud."

I wondered if perhaps money had been the stumbling block. But I didn't like to ask. Why else would a woman as clearly intelligent as Brenda have almost not made it?

The woman glanced around. "I taught most of the younger ones in this room. Nearly forty years I taught school here."

"That's a lot of years. And a lot of students. Do you remember all of them?"

She chuckled, and it was a husky sound. "I remember more than they wish I did for the most part. I can't always remember everyone's name now, but most of them. And the outstanding ones like Brenda I'll never forget."

As though she knew we were talking about her, Brenda looked over and smiled. And there was such a strong affection between these two women, I almost wished I'd gone to school here. Not that I'd had a bad time in school, but I was different, and being different in high school is social death.

Bridget Sullivan was hailed by another of her students, no doubt, and excused herself, and I quickly told Kathleen about the ghost in the mirror.

"That'll only be Billy," she said in a soothing voice. "He's likely not passed all the way over yet. He always enjoyed a party, but he'll be gone in the morning, I'm certain."

I lowered my voice. "It wasn't Billy. It was an old woman, and she didn't look friendly."

"I don't know who that is, but no doubt you've left yourself too open."

I couldn't believe she was blaming me.

"Give it fifteen more minutes, and we'll leave."

I was going to tell her I'd walk, but I suspected it would take me half an hour to walk back to the center of town from here. The sensible thing was to wait. Not knowing anyone to talk to, I drifted toward the window and looked out into the backyard. I wished I was in the overgrown garden and not in the company of a corpse, the ghost in the mirror and this heavy feeling that plagued me like bad indigestion.

There was a man standing out there smoking a cigarette. He caught my eye because he didn't seem to be coming toward the house or going away from it. I got the feeling he couldn't make up his mind which he was going to do. He had curly, black hair and a square face, a very stocky, muscular body. I bet he worked out constantly. Good-looking in a flashy way.

The cigarettes didn't match the heavy-duty working out, but maybe he was one of those occasional smokers.

He glanced up at the house, and I stepped back so he wouldn't catch me staring. Then he seemed to decide, threw his butt on the ground and ground it out with his shoe. If he'd made an effort to dress up, it was in the buttoned shirt he wore over his jeans. He took two steps toward the house, and then, to my surprise, I saw Brenda hurrying out to meet him.

I sensed anger coming from her. I didn't think he was consoling her. It looked to me like they were having an argument. Who argued with someone at their father's funeral? I didn't know what to do. It was so none of my business, but I was desperate for an excuse to get out of here. I could pretend I was leaving and make sure she was okay.

Kathleen was busy talking to a woman with a bad perm, so I went into the kitchen and slipped out the door. I walked down the back steps and headed toward the arguing pair. I heard Brenda say, "I don't care. You're not coming in."

He glowered at her. "I'm here to pay my respects."

She stood her ground, and every line of her body quivered with fury. "He wouldn't want you here either."

"How do you know that? You haven't been here. You don't know what's been going on."

"I know my father. He wouldn't want you here."

He reached out and grabbed her arm. "Brenda, I need to talk to you. It's important."

She yanked her arm back. "Let go of me."

I was so busy watching this drama unfold that I didn't even notice Bridget Sullivan, the teacher, had come out behind me. She muttered something and then strode toward the arguing pair. Unlike me, she hadn't stayed around to eavesdrop. She was wading right into the conflict. I could imagine her as a younger teacher getting instant discipline when she set her mind to it. She even sounded like a teacher when she said, "And what is the meaning of this, Jack?"

He dropped his swagger and instinctively straightened up. "Miss Sullivan. I hope you're well."

"Never mind all that. What are you doing here?"

His face settled into belligerent lines. "It's a wake, isn't it? I'm here to pay my respects to Mr. O'Donnell."

"I think Brenda would appreciate it if you would leave."

"But—"

"You can go and visit Billy O'Donnell in the graveyard if you've a mind to, once he's been laid to rest. But don't distress Brenda. Not today."

"I came here because I've got a few things I have to say to Brenda."

"Not now, Jack." Brenda turned away and headed back toward the house. I stepped behind a bush so that she wouldn't have to see me on her way past. It wasn't that I was cowardly, but some things you don't want witnessed, and I had a strong feeling that for her, that little encounter was one of them.

I stayed anyway, in case the eighty-year-old woman needed help against a guy that looked like a thug and a bully. But I should have had more faith in her. She said, "You go on home now, Jack."

"I have to talk to her. I've thought of nothing else since I got out of prison."

Well, that made me perk up my ears. What did the jailbird have to say to Brenda that was so important?

"She's got a different life now, Jack. And so do you."

"She owes me a hearing at least. And she knows it."

"Not here. Not now."

His face went dark. "You always sided with her. Teacher's pet."

She didn't rise to his bait. "You go on home now. Give your mother my best when you see her."

And, not really to my surprise, he turned around and slunk off. Bridget Sullivan stood there waiting until I heard an engine turning over, and then an old truck drove past us.

CHAPTER 3

*I*t felt like a hundred years before Kathleen and I
left the wake and headed back toward the high
street. We stopped at the intersection where the church stood.
I could see the grave was freshly dug, ready for Billy O'Donnell. And hanging over the wall of the graveyard was the yew
tree that had caused such consternation. I sat looking at it,
thinking the priest was right. Beautifully green branches
burst out everywhere as though waving for attention. The
bows overhung the graves, touched the church roof and, in
the other direction, arched over the road. It had a massive
trunk, twisted and wizened, and the branches that stretched
in all directions were as ragged as a torn umbrella.

She followed my gaze but must have thought I was
looking at the fresh hole in the ground. "Billy O'Connell will
be laid to rest tomorrow. The grave's all ready for him."

I told her what I had overheard about the yew tree,
between Father O'Flanagan and the red-haired guy who
didn't want to do the pruning.

The van idled as she nodded, not looking at all surprised.

"He's not been here so very long, Father O'Flanagan. It's best not to touch that tree."

I was surprised and showed it. "Why?"

"It goes back hundreds of years. The yew is a fine tree and known for its longevity and magic. And sure, that's lasted centuries. No one would dare take it down. It's survived thunder and lightning and droughts. Wars, pestilence. And still it stands." Her voice was hushed as though it were a mystic icon and not a simple tree.

Where I came from, we had trees that were a thousand years old. But they were massive cedars. And revered by the native peoples.

"The yew makes very nice wands and divining rods," she told me.

"But that tree could really use a prune. Look at the way it's hanging over those gravestones, and it must drop needles and bits of branch on the church roof. No wonder they're trying to raise money to fix the place up." I was no historian, but I thought the old church was beautiful and deserving of a little sprucing up, and that yew could definitely use a haircut.

"Well, if you're going to live here, I suppose you need to know the local legend."

"Okay. I'm game."

"There was an evil witch who lived in these parts."

I felt irritation prickle my skin. "Why do so many stories start with 'there was an evil witch'? It's so unfair, not to mention misogynistic."

"Well now, most times I would agree with you, but of course there are and always have been evil witches as well as the good ones. I do fear she was a bad one."

"What did she do? Cause the plague?"

She chuckled. "No, love. It seems she may have killed her husbands."

I turned to look at her. "Husbands? Plural?"

Kathleen seemed content to sit in the van and tell me the tale, which I had to admit sounded better by the side of a creepy old graveyard. "I believe there were several. She was reputed to have killed her husbands and done some other terrible deeds. She was tried and put to death."

I hated these kinds of stories. Too many innocent women had been hanged or burned for nothing more than being healers.

"The legend is that she was put in the ground upside-down, as they used to do, and with a heavy slab over her head. She was buried outside the church, of course, in unconsecrated ground."

"The locals really had it in for this woman."

"Indeed." We both stared at the tree. "But the next day she was seen again. She threatened to kill all the children if she wasn't paid vast ransoms from the townspeople. They killed her again and buried her, and her familiar with her, and this time the yew tree was planted over her with a spell upon it. So long as that tree stands above her, the evil witch cannot rise again."

I looked at the tree and then at Kathleen. "It's like reverse Snow White. Only instead of the young princess being trapped in a spell, it's the evil one."

"Evil indeed. So, while Father O'Flanagan might like to have the tree pruned, the locals don't want to do it. We're a superstitious lot, we Irish."

Coming from a witch, that was pretty rich.

"Well, I don't think you need to worry," I told her. "A

young guy named Archie didn't look like he was going to get anywhere near that yew."

She put her foot on the gas, and the grocery van began to move. There were still several hours of the work day left, and Kathleen had to go back to her grocery, and I would return to the bookstore.

As we drove, she said, "I wonder what will happen to the house now. He'll have left everything to his daughter, of course. But will she come back?"

"If she has a life in Dublin, why would she?"

"It's a fine, grand house."

"It's a fine, grand money pit. That place has beautiful bones, but it looks to me like it would take a fortune to bring it back to its glory days." Not to mention there was a ghost to get rid of.

"I know. Sad, isn't it? A place like that wants a family. Those rooms want people in them and parties and entertaining."

"I did not get the feeling that Brenda was planning to move back. In fact, she wants me to sell her father's books." My lack of enthusiasm must have shown in my tone.

"Well, I'm sure there'll be some good things in amongst the junk."

I hoped so. I suspected there would be a lot of garbage I'd have to wade through first.

"I overheard her tell Karen Tate that she was giving her all the bits and bobs that she might be able to sell to Granny's Drawers," Kathleen said. "I look forward to having a good rummage. Brenda's mother had some lovely things."

"Is that what people do here? Rummage through each other's things once they die?"

"It's a small town, dear. We find entertainment as we can."

WHEN I WALKED into the pub that night, I was glad Karen and I had decided to get together. I'd found the wake unsettling on its own, and then that scary-faced ghost or whatever it was peering at me from the mirror had seriously rattled me. I was glad to have some company other than my own and Cerridwen's. That cat definitely had her own agenda, and it was amazing how her outdoor roaming time so often coincided with my let's sit on the couch and snuggle time. Still, she was good company when she wanted to be.

However, a single woman close to my age who could keep up a conversation was probably better company and made me less likely to turn into the strange cat lady out in the cottage all alone.

The pub was surprisingly full, and I wondered how many other people had come here because they'd been to the wake earlier. I was right on time, but Karen was already there, and she waved to me from a quiet table for two in the corner. Perfect.

I walked over and sat across from her. "This is a brilliant idea," I said. "I really needed to get out."

"I feel the same way. What can I get you?"

I asked for a red wine, and she went over to the bar. Sean O'Grady and she chatted like old friends. No doubt they were old friends. And she returned not with two glasses of red wine but an entire bottle.

"Sean says if we don't drink it all, we can take it home." She grinned at me. "Though I doubt there'll be any left."

I wasn't a big drinker, but I agreed with her assessment. She poured and then lifted her glass in a toast. "Here's to female friendships."

We both sipped, and then she set her glass down. "How did you enjoy your first Irish wake?"

I couldn't tell her about the ghost in the mirror, obviously, so I paraphrased what Andrew Milsom had said, that at least in Ireland people didn't avoid the subject of death but celebrated it as a passage. Trite but true.

"I don't think I'd want a wake, personally," she said. "I don't want a load of people seeing me after I'm dead. I'd want them to remember me looking a bit more lively."

I had to agree.

We sipped wine, and while I frantically tried to think of a neutral topic of conversation, she proved herself much more adept at making a new friend. "Tell me all about Quinn Callahan."

I took another, fortifying sip of red wine. Before I got into get-to-know-you conversation, I wanted to clear the air. "Karen, I'm really sorry about what happened with Declan O'Connor. I didn't mean to throw you under the bus like that."

She looked taken aback at my bluntness. For a moment, she didn't say anything, and so I went on. "It seemed like the only way I could provoke a confession was to bring everything out into the open. But you were collateral damage, and I'm sorry."

She looked up at me, and her eyes were somber, thoughtful. "You did nothing wrong. We did. Me and Rosie Higgins. Certainly Declan O'Connor, who was the author of his own misfortunes if there ever was one." She settled back in her chair, one hand playing with the bottom of her wine glass. "Even now, I look back and I don't know how I could have been so stupid. You had to have known him. He wasn't much to look at. But the charm of the man. And, even though he was dreadfully unfaithful to his wife and to all of us, in his way, he was a good man. When he was with me, I think he really believed that he loved me and we'd end up together. And probably when he was with Rosie, it was the same. And his poor wife. Anyway, now I look back and I realize what a fool I made of myself. You didn't do it. I did it to myself."

I didn't disagree, but I also had sympathy. "What woman hasn't made a fool of herself over a man?"

She smiled and tipped her glass to mine until they clinked. "Living here isn't easy as a single woman. You'll find in a place where everyone knows your business, they particularly take an interest in you if you're different."

Oh, great. I knew how that felt.

"Most of the people live here because their families have been here forever. O'Donnells marry O'Learys, and their children marry each other, and everybody's cousin or uncle is related to everybody else. Being from outside makes you different. Being single makes you different."

She sounded as though she were speaking of herself as well as me. "Aren't you from here?" I asked her.

She shook her head. "I'm all the way from Skibbereen."

"Skibbereen." I only repeated it because I loved the way some of these Irish towns sounded. Skibbereen should be something that was made with chocolate, perhaps eaten around a campfire. Not a place where people actually lived. I didn't know much about County Cork geography, but I knew

Skibbereen was only a few miles away. "You don't count as a local?"

"Definitely not."

"What made you come here then?"

She got a faraway look on her face. "I needed a change."

I didn't want to pry. I wondered if we should think about ordering dinner. And then she told me she'd grown up in Skibbereen to a single mother. "There were only the two of us. Mum worked so hard. She never had much of a job. She was a waitress." She shook her head. "It's no wonder I ended up falling for a man like Declan O'Connor. I never had a father, you see. And Mum never had the kind of boyfriends who stuck. What role models have I had? So I make terrible choices like she did." She sounded so defeated.

"Look, what happened with Declan O'Connor was awful. But it wasn't your fault. You're still reasonably young. It's not too late."

She looked at me as though she didn't believe my words at all. I didn't really believe them either.

It seemed we had quite a bit in common. I told her that my dad had left when I was young too. I'd also grown up with only a mother. But I never felt deprived. And I wasn't sure that it had made me distrust men. In my case, I'd married a man who was meant to be my friend not my husband. When I got past the pain and anger of betrayal when he and my actual best friend ended up together, I realized they were perfect together. Somehow, we all ended up as friends. Maybe it was peculiar, but it had worked for us. Emily was still one of my best friends, and I missed her fiercely, as much as I missed her two daughters, who were the closest I'd ever get to children of my own.

She shook her head. A sparkle of anger lit her green eyes. "My dad didn't leave. He was never there. My mother claimed she didn't even know who he was." She shrugged. "And maybe she didn't. Based on the number of men who came through our doors, I wouldn't be a bit surprised."

She had definitely had a very different upbringing than I'd had. I wasn't entirely sure that it was not having a father that had made it so difficult for her, but more likely the instability of a chaotic home life. Sure, I'd love to know whatever happened to my dad. But he'd turned out to be the guy who disappears and forgets to send child support payments or birthday cards or anything else, which never made finding him a top priority.

He'd been around for my first twelve years, at least, but he was the first man who broke my heart. When he left, my mom was the best mom she knew how to be. When she'd died, I was still only a teenager. That had been bad. And probably why I'd ended up with Greg. He was calm and stable and decent. And there. There for me when I'd needed him.

Karen said, "You should look for your father. Look on one of those internet family tree database things. People are always looking for their lost fathers and children."

I'd honestly never thought about it. It was a good idea, except I wasn't sure I wanted to find my dad. What did I want with a man who would walk out on his family? I suspected I was better off without him. I said as much, and Karen's face grew still. "Sometimes you are better off not to know."

At the bitterness in her tone, I looked at her. "You found him, didn't you? Your dad."

She glanced up at me as though shocked I'd guessed, but

her face had pretty much given the game away. She nodded. "It wasn't the joyous reunion I'd dreamed of," she said, sarcasm dripping from the words. "He had another family."

"I'm so sorry."

Her shoulders went up and down once. "It's life, though, isn't it?"

"And, in spite of our crap childhoods, we survived," I reminded her. We clinked glasses again and decided to order dinner. Oysters and chips for her and bangers and mash for me. Because when did I ever get bangers and mash in Seattle?

We talked of other things, village gossip, and suddenly she said, "Have you got your eye on the doctor?"

I was so shocked I bit my tongue. Ow. "Have my eye on the doctor? Dr. Milsom?" It was a pretty good guess, as he was the only doctor in town.

"Yes. I saw you watching him at the wake."

I had been watching him. He'd been a friendly face in a crowd of people who treated me like an unexploded bomb. I was trying to come up with an answer when she continued. "A friendly warning. He's as walled up as a maximum security prison." Which made me suspect she had an interest there herself.

However, I was always curious about people's stories. "What happened?"

She leaned in. "I heard his wife left him for his best friend."

I could have laughed out loud. I knew that story only too well. But I kept my face suitably grave. "That sucks."

"Nobody ever sees him with a woman. Though he does go to Dublin and back to London occasionally, so who knows what he gets up to there. But if you've your eye set on being a country doctor's wife, I wouldn't get too invested."

"Duly noted."

In one of those awful coincidences, Andrew Milsom walked into the bar exactly then. He looked around as though checking on who was there and seeing us, waved. We both waved back, and I felt terrible that we'd been gossiping about him. Not that we'd said anything bad. I was only gleaning information on my new neighbors. He went up to the bar and ordered what I was beginning to recognize was his usual drink. Whiskey, neat. He got to chatting with the bartender and another man who was sitting up at the bar. I felt that Karen was watching him too. She said, "For eligible men around here that you might actually fancy, he's about it."

Her gaze roamed around the pub, and she pointed out Danny, who had to be seventy and seemed to spend most of his time hanging around in Finnegan's Grocery. "Or there's Danny. He's single, still has his teeth. Most of them, anyway."

I laughed. "Thanks. I'm fine for now."

"Have you ever tried that internet dating? That was a right waste of time."

"Who hasn't? And it wasn't any better in Seattle." That wasn't completely true. I had met some nice men. I'd had a couple of relationships, but I could never be totally honest. There was a reason witches were so often alone.

CHAPTER 4

*B*renda O'Donnell was as good as her word. Unfortunately. Only two days after she'd buried her father, an old Land Rover pulled up in front of my shop. Brenda got out, and I watched her open the back and haul a box of books out. With her was the young red-haired guy I'd seen telling Father O'Flanagan that he didn't want to touch that old yew tree. He must be one of those people around town that you could hire for odd jobs. I'd have to get his information. He was young and strong, and where she had one box of books in her arms, he stacked one on top of the other and came behind her bearing two. I rushed to the front door and opened it for them.

"Thanks," Brenda said, panting slightly.

I suspected she was just going to dump them at her feet right in the front of my store, and I couldn't have that. I said quickly, "Bring them through here, would you?"

She didn't look too pleased, but she followed me down one narrow corridor of books to the back, where it was slightly more open. She dropped the box with a thunk. Her companion was about to do the same. I was apologetic, but I said, "Could you take those upstairs? That's where I keep all the stock that I haven't dealt with yet."

"Happy to oblige," he said and staggered upstairs with the boxes. Brenda put a hand to her lower back and sighed. "I'm sorry. I cannot carry one more heavy item. Archie will have to bring the rest of the boxes. I feel like my back will break as it is. I push paper around all day. I'm not accustomed to manual labor."

I felt for her, but I also wished I could be so lucky. I used to be a paper-pusher and researcher myself. Now that I ran a bookshop, if I wasn't standing on my feet, I was hauling books around. And nobody who hasn't worked with books knows how heavy they are. Still, she'd just lost her dad, and I wanted to be compassionate.

Brenda O'Donnell looked absolutely worn out. I could see the dark circles under her eyes from lack of sleep, and strain made her face look pinched and pale. Was it only grief? Exhaustion too, I thought. "I'm sorry. I remember how it was when my mother died. So much to do and you can't think clearly."

She looked like she was verging on tears. "That's it exactly. I've got so much to do before I leave tomorrow. I don't know how I'll get everything done."

I didn't know what her situation was. Maybe she couldn't get any more time off work, which seemed brutal when she'd only buried her father a couple of days ago. Personally, I thought it would do her good to spend a bit of time in the place where she'd grown up and where he'd passed. But it wasn't any of my business. Maybe writing briefs and suing people was her way of coping.

Perhaps, if I hadn't recently suffered a loss myself, I would have turned her down. How many more books did my bookstore need? And, from a quick glance in the boxes that she had brought over, there was a lot of junk in there. On the other hand, my sudden move from Seattle to Ballydehag was still fresh in my memory. In two weeks I'd not only rented out my house, but I'd given away all my kitchen stuff and more than half of my furniture. I'd only kept the pieces that felt meaningful to me. Still, I'd filled a whole storage locker in Seattle. And I'd felt more than a little stressed by the whole experience. So I decided to do her a favor.

"Don't worry. Everything will turn out."

Her eyes shimmered with tears. "Thank you so much." Then she blinked them away, obviously feeling foolish at her sudden emotion. "I don't suppose you want a very large dining table and eight solid oak chairs, do you?"

I laughed. She must know as well as everybody else did that I lived in a tiny cottage. "Can't help you there." On impulse, I said, "Would you like a cup of tea?" She probably didn't have time, but sometimes a person needed a break. I could see the war going on in her face. She didn't have time, but the longing to sit in this pretty little bookstore and get off her feet for a few minutes won out. "I'd love that."

I didn't even offer her a choice of tea. I knew exactly what she needed. I had a fantastic, calming brew that I'd made myself. It contained chamomile, lavender, rose hips and a little valerian root, among other things. I went into my tiny kitchen and brewed tea. Then, making sure she wasn't looking, I waved my hand over the tea and whispered, "Let she who would sip this tea, calmness find, of anxiety be free. So I will, so mote it be."

I poured us both a cup because, frankly, I could use some calming myself. I picked up other people's emotions too easily. Always dangerous when they were in emotional crisis. It made me a good witch, but it didn't help my mental state.

I brought the tea over to the two comfy chairs with the small table between them that was just perfect for this purpose.

Cerridwen came padding down the stairs, looking displeased. She'd been snoozing upstairs on the couch, and having her sacred nap disturbed by a sweaty guy hauling boxes had not pleased her. No one can do miffed like a cat.

However, she was never one to miss a warm lap and the chance of a treat. She looked between the two of us. I suspected Cerridwen could sense emotion and knew she was needed. She jumped up onto Brenda's lap.

Not everybody was a cat person, so I was ready to grab Cerridwen off her lap and put her onto mine, but the woman beside me sighed and sank back. "What is it about a cat? They're just so comforting." Cerridwen obligingly began to purr.

I could feel the woman calming down. She took a sip of tea, and that helped even more. "This is delicious."

"It's a special brew of my own. I'll send you home with some."

"Do. It's magical."

I chuckled. She had no idea.

Kate O'Leary, the schoolteacher, came in, but she merely greeted us both when she saw us and went about her business browsing. Mrs. O'Leary was a very low-maintenance customer. She knew the shop almost as well as I did and liked to browse undisturbed.

I said, still thinking about that heavy dining suite, "What will you do with the house?"

"Well, I won't move back here, that's certain."

"It looks like a wonderful home," I said, almost to myself.

"Aye, it is that. But it's too big and far too much work. Besides, my life is in Dublin now."

"It would make a wonderful bed-and-breakfast," I said, thinking of that grand, old home fixed up and made welcoming. And cleansed of evil spirits.

"It would at that. But more likely it will be knocked down and made into some housing development. That's what usually happens with big, old houses. Catholics aren't having large families anymore. And nobody's got the money."

Mrs. O'Leary came out with four books. Two for herself and two for the school. I excused myself to ring up her purchases. Kate dropped her voice very low and said, "It's kind of you to take an interest in Brenda. She's had a hard time."

I had no idea what that was about. "I feel sorry for anyone who has to move in a hurry right after their father died."

When Brenda and I were settled once more with our tea, a plate of shortbread biscuits on the small table between us, Brenda said, "I haven't lived here for years. I'd forgotten what it's like with all the small-minded gossip and everyone knowing everyone else's business. I don't know how you can stand it after a city like Seattle. Ballydehag is so backward."

Even though I'd only been here a few weeks, I felt my hackles rise. I'd come to like this charming village. I mean, sure, you could look up quirky in the dictionary and there'd be a picture of Ballydehag staring back at you, but after I'd been booted out of the States by some very angry witches, I'd been offered a refuge here. One I badly needed. So to hear her trashing the place annoyed me. Which, I supposed, was the first step in turning into one of those backward locals.

"It's not so bad when you get used to it," I said.

Cerridwen made a contented sound and rolled over, exposing her belly to be rubbed, which left her head upside down from where she watched me out of half-closed eyes. Considering that she'd only adopted me a few weeks ago, I'd fallen in love.

I politely asked Brenda how it was going with the house cleanout.

She made a face. "It's a terrible job. I should have made my dad throw loads of that junk out over the years, but he was a stubborn old man. And he was convinced that all that rubbish would be valuable someday or he'd find a use for it. I suppose because he grew up in hard times, he never got over the idea that once something came into your life, it should never leave."

"Pack rats are the worst," I agreed.

"I've got boxes of stuff to go to Karen Tate at Granny's Drawers to sell, and I'll take as much of the good stuff back to Dublin as I can." She groaned. "And then I'll have to sort out selling the house."

"Isn't there anyone local who could help you? Old friends? Family?"

"No. I've been gone too long. My dad was never very close with his family. My mum's people live over in County Clare."

She sounded almost as rootless as I was. "I'm sorry. It's difficult not to have family at a time like this."

"Family isn't always a blessing. In my work, you wouldn't believe the fusses and troubles I see."

I smiled faintly. "One advantage to being an only child, I suppose."

"It is that."

As Archie staggered up the spiral staircase with yet another load of books, I glanced nervously up above me. Perhaps I should find a different place to store my extra stock. Would that upstairs floor hold with all this extra weight on it?

As though she'd read my thoughts, Brenda said, "I'm awfully grateful to you for taking all the books. I'm sure some of them must have a good resale value. No doubt some of them you'll just want to get rid of."

There was one more box of books that Archie hefted upstairs and then, looking hot, sweaty and exhausted, he staggered back down again. I felt so sorry for him, I offered him a cup of tea. He shook his head. "You wouldn't have some water, would you?"

I poured him a glass of my finest tap water, and he chugged it back gratefully.

Brenda hadn't drunk much of her tea, and I could tell she wasn't ready to go. I said, "Why don't you finish your tea and I can run you back home?"

"Oh, that would be heaven. Just five more minutes to rest with this sweet cat purring would be like a day at the spa. Archie, you can keep going with packing the van."

He nodded, and then with a cheerful wave, he headed out. Before he left, I asked him for his contact information. He didn't have a card, but, in a slightly panting tone, he gave me his details, which I punched into my phone. His name was Archie Mahoney, and he did odd jobs, though not, he insisted, anything with plumbing or electrical.

Living in an old cottage and running an old shop, I would likely need his help.

Brenda and I chatted for another twenty minutes or so while she finished her tea. Then, heaving a sigh, she said, "I wish I could stay in Ballydehag longer. My work load is crushing, or I'd take a bit of a break. Things are ... difficult right now."

"I'm sorry." I felt that she wanted someone to talk to, so I sat quietly and let her find the words. When she spoke, she seemed to be talking to Cerridwen, looking down at that sweet face. "It's a funny thing, moving away from home and making a new life." She glanced at me and then back at the cat. "As you know. I thought I could leave all the bad behind and begin anew. But I find myself repeating the same mistakes."

I thought about my attempt at a fresh start and how quickly I'd botched it, interfering where I shouldn't, again. Though I had solved a murder. Shouldn't that count for something?

I wondered what mistakes this very together-seeming woman had repeated. I didn't want to push. She'd tell me if and when she was ready.

She looked at me, and I saw the strain in her eyes. There was more there than tiredness. "Do you ever think we're all cursed with a particular failing, and whatever you do, however far you run, you'll still repeat the same patterns?"

"Oh, I hope not," I said. "But you're right. It's too easy to drag that heavy baggage with us when we should leave it behind or throw it overboard."

I sensed she was about to tell me what was on her mind when the shop door opened and two old women came in.

Clara McPherson and Edna O'Grady were regular browsers, mostly because they were retired and widowed with not much going on in their lives. They walked in chatting. Brenda made a sound of horror, and I knew exactly why. If those two found her here, they'd be over with condolences and a million nosy questions. I said, "Go out the back. My car's there. I'll be out in a minute."

"What about them?" she asked, standing and replacing Cerridwen in the chair's seat.

"They can stay and watch the shop for a few minutes. They'll be delighted."

I DROPPED Brenda back at the house. A small moving van was parked outside, its back doors open. She blew out a breath. "I'll be so glad when this is all behind me."

On impulse, I reached over and touched her hand. "When you get back home, take some time for yourself. Grief hits us in funny ways."

She looked startled at the intimacy, then nodded. Almost to herself, she said, "And not only grief."

On my way back, I passed the church, but it wasn't the old steeple I noticed or the enormous banner asking for donations for the restoration fund. What I saw was a truck with a telescoping arm with a bucket on the top. A man was standing inside the bucket with a chainsaw, pruning the old yew. This was a regular occurrence in bigger cities where the telephone line people worked on phone lines and city workers kept trees trimmed, but it was odd out here in the virtual middle of nowhere. The side of the truck said Cork

Tree Services. And there was a team of three working on the old yew tree beside the graveyard behind St. Patrick's.

Obviously, the locals couldn't be persuaded to prune the tree that was the stuff of legend, but Father O'Flanagan hadn't given up. He'd gone to Cork city to get a crew.

I pulled up at the side of the road and watched. I was simultaneously sad to see that grand, old tree that no one had dared touch for hundreds of years being attacked with a chainsaw and pruning shears, but also the practical side of me, the one that was a newcomer like the priest, could see the benefit in getting rid of some of the enormous branches that hung all the way across the road on one side and well into the graveyard on the other. I suspected that Father O'Flanagan had been right, and one good windstorm and that thing could cause a lot of damage. Of course, everyone in town would probably say that the tree had been standing there for hundreds of years without falling down yet.

There was no one about on an overcast weekday afternoon. I wondered if the priest had chosen this time deliberately so he could have the work done before the locals set up a protest.

I could see a cluster of smaller branches had fallen into the road. Kathleen had reminded me that yew wood was very good for wands and divining rods, and a tree this old would have power of its own. I pulled my car to the side and got out and walked over. The air smelled of fresh-cut wood, the piney scent of the old tree, earth and, oddly, I caught a whiff of body odor.

There was a branch, about two feet long, that hung balanced on the top of the old wall as though offering itself to me. I picked it up and immediately felt a tingle in my palm as though it were communicating with me. Nice. I ran my thumb along the dark green needles. There were even a few red berries on it. Once I'd dried the wood, I could work with it. I wasn't normally one to use wands. I'd found that all a wand really did was improve your focus, and mine was good. But it might be nice to experiment with a divining rod, and what better material than this legendary and historic piece of yew?

I put the branch on the passenger seat, then carried on my way.

When I got back to my shop, the sky was gray and dismal, and as the afternoon grew longer, rain began to fall. I was from Seattle, the Pacific Northwest, which was famous for its rains. But I'd rarely seen a rain like this. It was raining so hard the drops were bouncing up off the pavement, and soon the road was awash with little streams. I'd driven in this morning because rain was forecast. By the time five o'clock rolled around, it was gloomy and wet, and when I put my head out the front door past the awning, I was immediately soaked. No wonder I'd had no customers since Edna and Clara had left.

I went upstairs thinking I might as well at least have a look at those boxes Brenda and Archie had dropped off. I was in no hurry to drive home in a storm, and Cerridwen was happily sleeping on one of the chintz reading chairs.

I made my way up the spiral staircase and was pretty shocked at the sheer number of boxes that had come from Brenda O'Donnell. At least Archie had stacked them nice and neatly. And she'd labeled each one, for which I was grateful. I took a quick look. In black Sharpie she'd written, "books, history" and "books, hobbies and crafts" and "books, paperback thrillers and romance" and "books, possibly valuable."

Naturally, I chose to open that one first. I pulled it toward me. There was so much packing tape on there that I needed to go to my desk and get scissors and a box cutter. When I returned, I shook my head. I was like a little kid at Christmas going for the brightest, shiniest package first.

No. I would make myself do a couple of the most boring boxes, get those out of the way. No doubt I could very quickly have a junk pile, and I'd call Archie back and get him to take the books down again and probably all the way up to the recycling depot. Or maybe I could put some free boxes out in front of my store. If Kathleen was right, and the residents loved a good rummage, perhaps they'd like a literary rummage.

Maybe I could make it a charity where I'd raise a bit of money for the church's restoration campaign. I thought it would be a nice way to add something to the community.

So I began with the box labeled paperbacks, thriller and romance. Those seemed like the kind of books that somebody might give a few euros for, enjoy a nice read and also feel good about supporting the church restoration project.

Even as I opened the box, the smell of must hit me. As I went through the books, I started to laugh. These books might have been thrilling in the forties, but now they were more like relics of history. And as for the romances, most of them were of the doctor and nurse variety. Where the doctor was always male and superior, and the nurse was female and deferential. I shook my head. As a feminist, how could I even put these out? I pushed them to one side. Then I opened the next box of thrillers. These were more hopeful. They were all published within the last twenty years at least, many of them hardback. I pulled out an old John Grisham, but as I opened it, a dead moth fell out. In about ten minutes, I had ten books I'd keep for myself to sell and thirty books for the donation box out front, and another five or six were going straight to the recycling depot.

I worked steadily for a couple of hours and got to know Mr. O'Donnell. Digging through people's books is like digging through their psyches. I learned about his interests, his passions. And I could soon differentiate which books were his and which were his wife's. There were a few books that I suspected had belonged to Brenda growing up.

There was a very respectable set of Tolkien in hardcover that, from the date, I suspected had been Brenda's. I thought it was sad that she was giving the set away, but if she'd wanted it, she'd have taken it with her.

The Victorian women's novels had belonged to Brenda's mother, I thought. Also the books on feminism, probably the cooking and home decorating books, and perhaps the books on music.

I had at least a hundred books I could add to my shop's stock, and it was after seven. The rain had eased up a bit, so I could get home and get some dinner. I would definitely need a bath after handling all these dusty books. Cerridwen snoozed contentedly on the couch in the upstairs office, and the rain drumming softly against the roof reminded me so much of Seattle that I felt oddly at home.

Okay, I decided that I had earned my prize. The box of books she considered possibly valuable. This was a woman who had a full set of hardcover Tolkiens and hadn't considered those valuable. I wondered what she considered a treasure.

With some eagerness, I ripped into the box.

On top was a note: "Mother collected books by female Irish authors." Oh, good. I could put more books in my local authors section. I scanned through and found some lovely hardcovers by Elizabeth Bowen, Iris Murdoch and authors I'd never heard of but should probably read. I suspected some of these would turn out to be first editions and possibly valuable.

I stacked them neatly on a table. Beneath the Irish women was a copy of The House at Pooh Corner, the second of the Winnie-the-Pooh novels. Just looking at the book, bound in green cloth, made me smile. I'd loved those books as a child. I had a look at the copyright page. This copy had been published by Methuen in 1928. I sucked in my breath. This was a first edition of the famous children's book written by A.A. Milne and illustrated by E.H. Shepard. If I was right, it was worth thousands.

If the Milne was a first edition, I'd give it back to Brenda. This was one of her father's treasures, for sure, and I couldn't keep it knowing she'd given away something unaware of its true value.

I continued through the box, feeling that I was finally being rewarded for my kindness in letting her dump all this junk on me, as I discovered two Ian Flemings, one signed by the author. I'd have to return that to Brenda, too. It would be worth a lot.

At the bottom of the box was a thick book wrapped in cloth. That was odd. I drew it out, and as I unwrapped it, my fingertips began to tingle. What emerged was a leather-bound book that looked ancient. Another treasure? I opened the cover. And discovered that this was a handwritten manuscript. I opened it carefully, turning the pages as though they were infinitely precious, not because they had monetary value. This was a book of shadows.

A witch had left this behind. There was no date on it, but given the type of paper, the ink and the general condition made me suspect it was very old. Perhaps hundreds of years old. Unfortunately, I couldn't read any of the spells because it was in Gaelic.

This was a treasure indeed. As was the A.A. Milne and the signed copy of Casino Royale. Brenda had probably been so busy shoving books in boxes that she'd stopped paying attention. I didn't blame her being completely overwhelmed, but I would blame myself if I took advantage. At least two books were worth a lot of money. The book of shadows was a valuable collector's item.

As a witch, I would love to get it translated and find out what was in it. What secrets did it tell? But I couldn't. I had to return this.

CHAPTER 5

The rain had let up now to barely a sprinkle, and I was getting hungry. I'd take the valuable books back to Brenda on my way home. I didn't even want books worth that much money stored in my shop overnight. It made me nervous. Besides, she'd said she was leaving in the morning. I didn't want to miss her.

When I put my coat on, Cerridwen rose on her paws and stretched her back out, then gave an enormous yawn before hopping off the chair and following me. I made sure the lights were all out and the front door locked and then let myself out the back. My little car was drenched, poor thing. I opened the passenger door, and Cerridwen didn't need an invitation to jump up quickly to avoid getting wet. I walked around and settled myself behind the wheel. I muttered a quick protection spell, as I always did when I was driving. Not so much for myself, but for anyone else unlucky enough to be on the road at the same time as me.

I backed out carefully into the little lane, then headed toward Brenda O'Donnell's house. It didn't take more than seven minutes to get there. The windshield wipers were scraping on the windshield now as the rain had eased up to almost nothing. When I pulled up in front of the O'Donnell house, I noticed the white van still parked in front with its back doors open and more furniture and boxes partly loaded.

I got out of the car and stared at the house. That place still gave me the creeps. I wouldn't stay. I wouldn't even go inside. I'd bang on the door, give Brenda's books back, or at least make some arrangement whereby I might sell them and give her the proceeds, all but a small commission.

There were lights on in the house and, leaving Cerridwen in the car, I picked up the bag with the valuable books in it and hurried up the path to the front door. I banged on it. No one answered. I knew she was there because I'd seen the lights on, the van half loaded, and in front of it was the battered Land Rover. Was there a bell? I found it and pressed the doorbell. I could hear it ringing inside. No doubt she was up on another floor and couldn't hear me knocking. Again, nothing. That was odd. I was tempted to get in my car and drive away, but I'd come this far and I was certain she was inside. I walked around to the kitchen door. It was open. I knocked against the open door and called out, "Hello?"

Then I heard footsteps banging as though someone was racing down the stairs. What on earth?

Before I could even take in that the banging footsteps were far too heavy to belong to Brenda O'Donnell, Archie burst into the kitchen. He looked wild-eyed, and his hair was all over the place. He saw me and yelled, "Help. I don't know what to do. She's fallen down."

I immediately grew calm. Well, somebody had to be. And Archie clearly wasn't the man you wanted in an emergency.

"I've got to call 999. She's hurt."

The first thing I had to do was calm him down before he fainted. "Take a breath." He couldn't. He was near passing out. His color was heightened, and he was hyperventilating. "Archie. Look in my eyes." I kept my voice deliberately calm. And when he finally looked at me, I said, soothingly and calmly, "Archie, you're feeling calmer now. Breathe in with me and breathe out with me." He did. And we repeated the exercise until he was calm enough to tell me what was going on.

"It's Brenda. She's upstairs on the floor."

"Did she fall? Is she sick?"

"I don't know. There was blood. She wasn't moving." Oh, that did not sound good.

He was trembling all over. "I don't want to go back there."

I was already moving. "Call 999," I said.

I heard him make the call as I ran through the house to the stairs. The rooms were shockingly bare after the chaos of clutter at the wake. The junk and knickknacks were gone, as was most of the furniture. There were boxes everywhere, neatly labeled and stacked.

I didn't see any sign of Brenda, so I ran up the stairs. "Brenda," I called out. There was no answer.

Oh, dear. I felt that shadowing heaviness.

I found her in the master bedroom. It was the biggest room at the front of the house, no doubt the room where her father had breathed his last. She was on the floor on her side. One hand reached out. I thought she'd been reaching toward the old telephone that was still on the stand beside the bed. I didn't need the doctor to figure out what had felled her. There was a massive gash in the back of her head and a brass candlestick on the ground. Someone had hit her very hard.

I sank to my knees at her side. "Brenda?" I called out softly. I put my hand to her forehead and found it warm. Oh, good. She wasn't dead. She moaned. It was soft, but she'd made a sound.

"Stay with me, Brenda. I'm getting help. You'll be all right."

I knew Archie had called the ambulance, but I grabbed my cell phone and called Dr. Drew Milsom. He picked up right away, and I explained what was going on. He said, "Stay with her. I'm on my way."

He didn't need to worry. I would hardly leave her. I ran to the door and yelled down to Archie to keep an eye open for the ambulance and police and bring them straight up as soon as they arrived. "Will do," he called up in a wavery voice.

I thought he'd be better with a proper job to do, even if it was just watching out for the ambulance. I strained my ears for the sound of sirens as I ran back and spoke soothing words to Brenda. "The ambulance is on its way, Brenda. We'll get you to the hospital. You'll be all right."

I didn't believe my words. I didn't think she would be all right. Her skull was bashed in and still bleeding sluggishly. I hoped doctors could save her even as I felt her slipping away. Death doesn't always take a person all at once. Sometimes it pulls them slowly to the other side. Brenda was young and in the prime of life. I could feel the way she was clinging to life. Fighting for it. And I was cheering her on in that fight. I took her hand in mine. Oh, I was tempted, but only for a nanosecond, to use the spell that I knew could hold her to life. I thought, even if I could keep her alive until help arrived, that would be okay, wouldn't it? But even as the idea crossed my mind, I squashed it. I had learned that lesson the hard way. I could do everything humanly possible to help Brenda cling to life, but I couldn't use magic.

She whispered, "Water," in a soft, reedy voice, but the word was clear.

"I'll get you some. I'll be right back."

If she wanted water, that had to be a good sign, didn't it? I ran into the bathroom. There must be a glass, even if it was just a toothbrush glass. I turned on the tap and found a water glass by the side of the sink. I filled it and then, as I turned to go, I noticed writing on the mirror.

In crude letters formed in some substance that looked like blood but was probably red lipstick, someone had written, "Go away. You're not wanted here."

I didn't have time to stand there and analyze the horrifying message. I took the glass back to Brenda. By the time I got there, her eyes were closed. Her breathing was shallow. "Brenda, I've brought you water," I said. She didn't answer. I took her hand in both of mine. I kept talking to her. I reminded her that help was on the way and that soon she'd be feeling better.

I heard the sirens now and told her that. I don't even know what I said. I just kept talking even as I could feel her life force fading. Then, thankfully, I heard the sounds I had been listening for so keenly. Male voices downstairs and then footsteps running up. Andrew Milsom came into the room, took one look at me, gave me a curt nod and strode over. I moved away so he could take my place beside Brenda.

"Ambulance is pulling up now," he said as he knelt at her side.

Now that a doctor was here, I could fall apart a little. She'd been fully alive and drinking tea with me what, four hours ago? Maybe five? So full of plans, in a hurry to get back to Dublin.

Brenda O'Donnell would not be going to Dublin tomorrow. She wouldn't be going anywhere.

The paramedics arrived then, with a stretcher. I couldn't watch this part, so I went downstairs. Archie was holding the door open, and two uniformed Gardaí walked in. "She's upstairs," Archie said, pointing.

One began running up the stairs. The second said, "Who found her?"

Archie gulped. "I did."

She said, "Go in the front room." He shot me a scared look and complied. Then she turned to me. "And you are?"

"Quinn Callahan. I came to drop something off and Archie told me Brenda was hurt. I went upstairs and stayed with her until the paramedics arrived."

"Go sit with your friend."

Archie was in the dining room, as the front-room furniture was all loaded and poor Brenda had yet to dispose of the dining room suite. The big, old-fashioned oak table with its eight chairs and the matching cabinets filled the room. The cabinets were empty now, and the surface of the buffet cleared, but at least we could sit.

Archie was running his thumbnail along a crack in the dining table, back and forth as though the movement soothed him. "Will Brenda live?" he asked in a trembling voice. He swallowed, and his Adam's apple bounced up and down as though it had better places to be.

"I don't know." I couldn't make sense of it all. "What happened?"

He turned to me, looking wild-eyed. "I went for my dinner break. Brenda told me to. She said she had to meet someone, so we'd take an hour and meet back here."

"Did she say who she was meeting?"

"No. And it wasn't my place to ask."

I nibbled my lip. At least thinking about who might have done this to Brenda helped keep my mind occupied. "Was she meeting them here or going out to meet them?"

He shrugged. "Dunno. I thought she was going out. There's no food in the house, but maybe she was meeting someone here."

She'd been attacked upstairs, but whoever she met could have come back with her. Perhaps with violence on their mind.

There was a clatter of footsteps on the stairs and someone calling out instructions. I was pretty sure they were taking Brenda away on a stretcher. Andrew Milsom popped his head in to tell us he was going along in the ambulance. "We'll do our best to save her," he said.

A police tech asked if we'd volunteer to be fingerprinted so they could work out whose fingerprints were whose upstairs in the master bedroom. We both agreed. She took our fingerprints and then gave us some packaged wipes.

It felt like a murder investigation. But Brenda wasn't dead, I reminded myself. However, she wasn't far from it. I thought it would be a miracle if she survived, but miracles happened.

The bathroom! The awful message. "Did you check the bathroom?" I asked.

She glanced at me oddly. "No. Not yet." She rose. "Stay here. An officer will be along shortly."

Archie and I sat in miserable silence in the dining room that I'd last been in for Billy O'Donnell's wake.

I hadn't enjoyed my time in this house then, and I enjoyed it even less now, waiting for the Gardaí and hoping against hope that Brenda would pull through.

Archie and I made labored conversation for a few minutes, and then both of us just gave it up and sat there, sitting silently with our own thoughts. After about twenty minutes, a young Garda took our statements. Mainly, they only wanted the barest details and our names and contact information. We were both asked to go down to the station the next day and make a full statement.

"Can we go now?" I asked. Cerridwen was still in the car and I felt burdened by pain, sadness and grief, as though the house itself were mourning.

"Let me find out for you," and he went back upstairs.

There was a knock on the front door. Archie jumped like a frightened rabbit, and his fair skin blushed under his red hair. His blue eyes opened so wide, I was afraid the eyeballs would fall out and roll onto the dirty carpet. To reassure him I said, "It'll only be more police. Someone must have locked the door by accident. I'll get it."

I opened the door, and standing in front of me was a stranger, not in uniform. He was about forty, with stylish, short hair, a beautiful suit and shiny, black shoes. He was good-looking in a boyish way. Something about him reminded me of my ex-husband, Greg. "Hello?" I said, waiting for him to pull out his identification.

He looked puzzled. "Hello."

There was a beat of silence as we both looked at each other. "Who are you?" I asked finally.

He looked down at his phone. Stepped back and checked the number on the house. "I feel I should ask you that question," he said to me with a humorous expression on his face.

"You're not with the police?"

He glanced around him. "Is this some sort of joke?"

Oh, dear. One of us had made a terrible mistake. "Are you looking for Brenda?" I asked him.

"Yes. Are you her friend?" He began to look concerned, no doubt beginning to suspect that the police cars had been called to this address. "Where is she?"

So not the question I wanted to answer right now. We stared at each other again and, perhaps because I was in the house and he was outside, he ceded me the upper hand. He said, "I'm Dylan McAuliffe." He looked at me as though I should know who that was.

"Okay. And you know Brenda how?"

"We're engaged." When I continued to stare, he said, "To be married."

He was her fiancé, and he hadn't been at her father's wake. I'd have remembered him. I had to ask. "Why didn't I see you at her father's wake if you're engaged?"

"Because I had to work. I wanted to be there, to support Brenda, of course I did. But I had to work, and she understood. I've come down here to help her move."

Not in those clothes. It was one reason he reminded me of Greg. That suit was tailored. The shoes were Italian and looked handmade, and when he'd lifted his cell phone, I'd seen his watch. It was a ten-thousand-dollar watch.

Whatever his job was, it paid well. And if he'd come to help Brenda move, he'd timed it for when the hard work would all be done.

"There are Gardaí vehicles out on the street. What is going on?"

Archie came to the door then, and his Adam's apple bounced up and down once more. "They said we can go.." He looked at Dylan McAuliffe. "Are you with the Guards?"

Dylan McAuliffe looked between Archie and me. "What's going on? Why does everyone think I'm a Garda?"

Archie and I exchanged glances, and clearly neither of us knew what to say. Finally, I said, "I'm sorry to tell you this, but Brenda's had an accident."

He looked stunned. "Accident? What kind of accident? Like a car wreck?"

I shook my head. "She's on her way to the hospital."

He glanced up as though all the noise upstairs was beginning to register and he was associating it with Brenda's injury. He seemed to wilt. "How badly is she hurt?"

"It's bad." It was all I could say. I wasn't going to lie to the man.

He took a step forward as though he'd push past me and go upstairs to her. "Where is she? We're to be married. I have to go to her."

"She's on her way to the hospital." I'd already said that, but I understood that shock made it hard to take in new information.

"Where?"

"In Cork. It's a tricky road," Archie said. "It can be difficult to find."

"Give me the coordinates. I'll put it into my GPS." His hands were shaking so badly, he couldn't manage it.

"Did you drive down from Dublin today?" I asked him.

He glanced up impatiently, as though it was irrelevant. "I did. Now, if you'll give me even the name of the hospital, I'll be on my way."

If he'd driven down from Dublin today and now had this horrific news, I couldn't let him drive to Cork on his own. I looked at Archie. "You know the way, Archie. Could you drive Dylan to the hospital?"

Archie looked so relieved to get out of the house that he nodded enthusiastically. "Excellent idea. My car is across the street. I'd be happy to drive you."

A shiny, late-model BMW was parked in front of the house, and across the street was a dusty, faded Skoda.

Dylan looked like he might argue, and then I said, "Trust me, it'll be faster."

I had no idea whether it would be faster or not, but I didn't think Dylan should be driving alone. I didn't know what news he'd get when he got to the hospital, but even if he could get there okay, I suspected that it might be terrible news that would greet him and he'd be better to have a driver on the way home. Maybe if he hadn't reminded me so much of my dead ex-husband, I wouldn't have been so concerned about him. As Dylan McAuliffe followed Archie out, I thought again how very dapper he was. Was he trying to impress others or himself?

I watched them drive away. I didn't want to interrupt all the activity upstairs, but had they checked the bathroom?

Surely the go away message was an important clue. I decided to wait until someone came down as I really didn't want to go back upstairs. The evening was relatively warm, so I left the door open and sat on the front step.

I was thinking about Brenda, wondering how she was making out, when a nondescript car pulled up. Out stepped two men I knew, Detective Inspector Walsh and his sidekick Sergeant Kelly.

If they were surprised to see me, they didn't show it. I stood as they grew closer. DI Walsh looked at me with those boxer's eyes. His looks hadn't improved since he'd last been in Ballydehag investigating a murder. He still looked like he'd lost a few too many rounds in the boxing ring. "Ms. Callahan," he said, emphasizing the Ms.

"Detective Inspector Walsh." I motioned behind me. "Everyone's upstairs."

His face never changed expression, but his eyes were sharp on mine. "Wait here."

I knew they were here because it was a crime scene, but I wondered whether they were already treating this as a murder investigation. Oh, poor Brenda. I hoped not.

The two detectives went upstairs. I stayed where I was.

I sat outside on the steps until the two detectives came down and found me there. "Exactly what did you see when you got here?" Detective Walsh asked.

I went through it one more time. "But who would hurt her? Who would do such a thing?"

DI Walsh wasn't one to crack a smile, but there was a slight shifting in his expression. "That's what we're here to find out."

I went through everything I could remember. "And did you see the bathroom?"

They looked at each other and then looked at me. "What about the bathroom?"

Presumably they'd been so busy in the bedroom where she'd been attacked, they hadn't bothered to search the bathroom upstairs. "The writing on the mirror. The warning."

"What warning?"

Really, I should join the Guards myself. I stood up. "Come on. I'll show you."

I went upstairs, and the two followed me. I led them into the bathroom, though only DI Kelly followed me inside. The mirror was clean, sparkling, so it really stood out in the dingy room. I turned to him. "Did someone clean it off?"

He looked at me like I'd been hit on the head. Of course, the police wouldn't rub away crucial evidence. But where was it?

"What exactly did you see?"

"The writing. It was right there on the mirror. In something red. I thought at first it was blood, but I think it was lipstick." I was starting to doubt myself. "Someone must have slipped in and wiped the mirror clean." I shivered at the thought that whoever had done it had been here while I was. Had they been hiding while I had called for help? If I'd stumbled on them, would I now be lying on a stretcher on my way to the hospital?

"What did the message say?" DI Kelly asked.

"Go home. You're not wanted here." Was I crazy? Seeing things that weren't there?

Or was I not going crazy? Was there another explanation for the writing on the mirror? I had assumed that message was directed at Brenda and somebody was telling her to go back to Dublin. Now I wondered if the message was intended for me. Some ancient and evil witch wanted me out of her way. Heat crawled up my neck. Finally, I said, "I'm so sorry. I think the shock and stress got to me."

"So you didn't see writing on the mirror?"

Well, I had, but I couldn't prove it. And they certainly weren't going to believe that a supernatural being had done it. I'd be far better to keep what little credibility I had left and keep my mouth shut.

"I think I'd better get home and lie down," I told them.

"Would you like a ride?" DI Walsh asked.

I appreciated the kindness but told him no. DI Walsh reminded me to go to the station in the morning and give a statement. I said I would and was allowed to leave. The bag of books I'd intended to return to Brenda was on the kitchen floor where I'd dropped them. I didn't want to leave them in an empty house, as they were so valuable. I'd hang onto them until Brenda was better or ... well, I'd hang onto them.

I made my way back outside, got into my little car and headed home. The cottage looked bedraggled in the rain, especially the roses, which were dripping and drooping. I picked up the books and the piece of yew I'd taken off the street what felt like days ago and was only a few hours, then I let Cerridwen out of the back, where she'd been curled up sleeping. She yawned, looked at the rain and scampered to her cat door.

When I got inside, I lit the fire for comfort as well as warmth.

The first thing I did was wash my hands under scorching water, scrubbing my nails. Then I brewed myself a pot of my calming tea and sat in the front room watching the restless waves. I knew I should eat something, but my stomach felt queasy.

About nine thirty, my phone rang. It was Andrew Milsom. "Quinn. I wanted you to hear it from me." And I knew before he told me that the news was bad. I could hear it in the heaviness of every word. "She didn't make it. I'm so sorry."

How many times had this man had to deliver the news that somebody's loved one hadn't made it? No wonder he'd retreated to what had seemed to be a peaceful village in Ireland, where the biggest thing he had to worry about was coughs and colds and when the fish might be biting. Instead, he'd been faced with murder.

Outside, I heard the restless sea sounding like quiet sobbing. Or maybe that was coming from inside me. "I'm sorry too."

There was a pause. "You've had a shock. Will you be all right?"

That was an interesting question. I didn't know. I felt strange and unsettled.

Brenda was now a murder victim.

CHAPTER 6

I took the books I'd intended to give Brenda out of the bag and set them on the table in the living room. I was puzzled as to what to do with them. I supposed until her will was read, I wouldn't know who the next of kin was. In the meantime, I wondered if I should get the books valued. Maybe I was wrong and a very old book of shadows was a curiosity rather than a treasure.

There'd been a vampire who'd come to the bookshop a few weeks ago. Rafe something. He was an antiquarian book dealer and a friend of Lochlan's. If anyone could tell me the value of these books, it would be him.

I'd meant to put the yew branch in the shed behind the cottage where I dried herbs, but with the rain, I'd beelined straight for the cottage door. I placed the branch above the fireplace where it lent a festive touch. A yuletide note creeping into the wet June day.

I settled myself in my favorite chair in the living room, which I suspected had also been Lucinda's favorite, as it offered a view of the ocean and there was a reading lamp by the side.

I got my reading glasses and tea and settled myself in the chair with the old grimoire. I'd told Drew I'd be fine and thanked him for letting me know Brenda was gone, but I was far from fine. I puzzled over that note on the mirror that had disappeared, and I worried that it might be connected with Brenda's death.

I sat for a long time with Cerridwen curled up in my lap. As though she knew I needed the comfort, or because of the rain, she'd stayed in.

I didn't speak Gaelic, but I loved the feel of the old book, and I tried to imagine who might have owned it, what spells this book might contain.

The pages were remarkably well-preserved for their age. Very little foxing, no sign of insect damage, and while the spine was loose and the leather cover scuffed and worn, the paper itself was in good shape and the old writing legible. No doubt the witch had made sure of it. I turned the pages slowly. I could see some pencil drawings of herbs and the odd note in a cramped hand.

There was one page that contained some familiar words. This spell wasn't in Gaelic but an older form of English. I said the words aloud, not at all sure of the pronunciation, but loving the sound of the words in the quiet room.

As I wicche be and by my crafte of sorserie

So I pleye to ouyrcome alle

Bewitchen him that bereth my herte

To that same Journey's end

I wasn't entirely sure what I'd said. It wasn't Gaelic, and it wasn't common English. I thought it might be something like Chaucer. Was that Middle English?

About eleven, Cerridwen got off my lap and stared, letting me know it was time for bed, and then she padded up the stairs.

I found it rather amusing that she kept whatever hours she liked, but when she was home at eleven, she liked me to go to bed.

She was probably right. There was no point sitting up late. I closed the grimoire and placed it carefully on the table. Then I turned out the lights and, as I generally did, paused to look out the window. The sight of the ocean was different every time I looked out. The moon waxed and waned. The waves were sometimes choppy and fierce, sometimes calm and lulling. The night might be clear or it might be clouded, and always I looked over at that solitary castle that Lochlan Balfour and a nest of vampires called home. There were lights on. I suspected that while my day was ending theirs was just beginning.

When I got upstairs, I found Cerridwen stretched out across the bed. For a small cat, she could take up a lot of real estate. I got myself ready for bed and then crawled in gingerly, trying not to disturb the cat. Her purring was the last sound I heard before I went to sleep.

I woke and opened my eyes. It was full dark, which was strange because there'd been moonlight last night, and I hadn't drawn the curtains. I rarely did. I liked to wake up to the morning light. If the weather was nice, I would open the balcony doors and welcome the morning.

I yawned and squinted at the clock. It must be the middle

of the night. The clock said seven-thirty. That was strange. Why was it so dark?

The cat was still sound asleep, curled in a ball in the bent crook of my knees. I eased myself out of bed and padded barefoot across the floor to the balcony doors. There was something black across the panes of the window door. What could it be? I put my face right up against the window and peered, but it was so dark I couldn't see anything. I turned on the light in the bedroom and then peered again.

I blinked and felt the first stirrings of unease. I was too sleepy for fear, but my foggy pre-coffee brain was still registering that something was wrong. It was like being inside an impenetrable forest. On the other side of the glass was what looked like tree boughs with thorns. Was I asleep and dreaming?

I pinched my arm and felt a sharp twinge. Not dreaming then.

I tried to open the doors, but they were stuck fast.

I was trying not to panic, but my heart was speeding up. I grabbed my housecoat and put on my slippers. Maybe something had happened in the night—a tree had fallen on the roof and I hadn't heard it. I'd have to go out and investigate. I went downstairs into the kitchen and, naturally, the first thing I did was look at the windows. Every one of them was black. I ran for the back door. I literally ran. I yanked and yanked, and I couldn't open the door.

I went to the front window, the largest one, and it looked like a million snakes, and they were moving. They weren't snakes, but branches. My entire cottage seemed to be wrapped in branches and thorns. And why were they moving?

Frantic now, I tried the front door. Nothing. I pulled and yanked. I tried a spell. I couldn't focus. I was too panicky.

I had to calm down. By this time, all the commotion had woken Cerridwen. She came trotting down and took a slow walk around the house. She must have been as unnerved as I was, for she went straight for her cat door. She butted her head against it and then turned to look at me as though it was my fault she couldn't get out. "I'm as stuck as you are," I told her.

I was weirdly glad that at least I had my cat for company. But I had to get out of here. Was there even enough air? It looked like it was vegetable, whatever was surrounding the cottage.

I calmed myself and then cast a spell to open a locked door. Nothing. I heard a scraping noise and realized it was the thorns scratching the window pane as the foliage wrapped tighter around my cottage. I could think of no spell that would break this curse, and I suspected my magic wasn't strong enough on its own.

There was only one person I could think of to call.

"You're up bright and early, Quinn," Kathleen said when she answered the phone. Then, as I babbled, she said, "Slowly, now. What's wrong?"

I told her about my problem, and she sounded quite surprised, as well she might. "You say there're thorns and branches all around your cottage?"

"I think they're thorns. It's hard to tell because I'm seeing them from the inside, and it's pitch black in here because there's no light coming in the windows. I can only see from the lights I'm turning on inside the house. They're moving. I think wrapping the cottage tighter and tighter."

"What have you been doing? Has somebody put a curse on you?"

"The only other witch I know is you. Have you put a curse on me?"

"Of course, I haven't."

"I'm kind of panicking here. I can't get out." And I didn't want to die by being squeezed to death by tree branches.

"Hang on a minute. I'll drive right over."

"Hurry."

Not knowing what else to do, I put coffee on. Even in this dire situation with my cottage wrapped around with branches and thorns, my body still craved caffeine. Probably even more so. While that was brewing, I ran upstairs to get dressed. Assuming that Kathleen could somehow break through, I didn't want her to find me in my nightclothes. I put on jeans and a T-shirt. I found a long-sleeved denim shirt. If worse came to worst and I had to hack my way out of here, I wanted to have sturdy clothing on.

I was drinking my first cup of coffee, staring in absolute bewilderment at the impenetrable greenery, when someone shouted my name. It wasn't Kathleen; it was a man. "Quinn? Are you all right?"

"Lochlan." He must have seen whatever was going on from the outside from the castle. I shouted that I was okay but that I couldn't get out.

"I'm not surprised. Your cottage is wrapped around in thick branches and thorns."

"How thick are they?"

"Hard to tell," he shouted back.

Then I spied the yew branch still sitting on the mantel

above the fireplace. No! "Lochlan?" I shouted. "Does it look like yew?"

"Now you mention it, it does."

I felt incredibly foolish, but I explained to him how I'd brought a piece of the yew tree home, and I suspected it had magical qualities.

"That may have been a mistake," he said. Understatement of the century.

"I've got a friend coming. Why don't you go on home, and I'll call you if I need you."

"I can get some chainsaws going, hire some people to cut you out of there."

I heard the sound of breaking glass. It was coming from upstairs. I screamed.

"Hold on," Lochlan said. "I'm coming to get you."

CHAPTER 7

"*T*hank you," I said in a trembling voice. I didn't want him to leave. I didn't want to be alone here. "I'm getting a little panicky."

He didn't say anything else, but I heard sounds from outside, though they were muffled by the thick branches and vines and thorns covering my windows. "What's going on?" I called out.

"Give me a minute." It was Lochlan's voice again, and he sounded out of breath. When had I ever heard him out of breath?

He was using some kind of tool, and I could tell that he was hacking away at the branches in front of my kitchen door. Oh, thank goodness. I'd always read that vampires had superhuman powers, and it sounded like those rumors were true.

I heard grunting and then tearing and crashing, and then suddenly my kitchen door flew open and Lochlan came inside. He looked a mess, and his normally meticulous clothes were covered in brambles and burrs. There were scratches on his hands and face. I went toward him. "Are you okay?"

I felt so grateful that he'd torn through some magical force to get to me. I felt like sleeping beauty. If he kissed me, what would happen? But instead of a delicate, young maiden and a handsome prince, we were a middle-aged witch and a vampire. I suspected the fairy tale would have a very different ending.

Anyway, I didn't think either of us had kissing on our minds. "Let's get you out of here," he said. I heartily agreed, but when we turned back, the door was once again shut and stuck fast.

Lochlan threw his weight against it, but it didn't budge. "I can't believe this. What happened? That is some powerful magic."

Tell me about it. I shook my head, as puzzled as he was. "I am not this powerful."

I went into the front room and retrieved the yew branch. "There were tree surgeons pruning the big tree behind the graveyard. I brought a branch home."

He looked at me, astonished. "You mean the great magic yew that has trapped evil for centuries?"

How many ancient yews were there in the town that had magical powers? "Yes. That yew."

"Are you crazy, woman?"

"You're stuck in here with me. I don't think I'm the only crazy one."

Our argument might have escalated, but Cerridwen was so excited to see Lochlan that he had to bend and pick her up. Already I noticed his scratches and wounds were healing. If it weren't for the mess all over his clothes, you'd never know he'd torn through an impenetrable forest to get to me.

I didn't know what to do with a vampire trapped in my cottage. "Do you want some coffee?"

He looked at me and shook his head. No doubt coffee was not his beverage of choice. I couldn't offer him anything he wanted. And I very much hoped he'd eaten before he arrived here.

My phone rang again. It was Kathleen. "I've never seen anything like it," she said when I answered. "I've snapped a photograph for you. It's as though a tree has grown up all around your cottage. You wouldn't know there was a cottage there."

I told her about the yew tree. "I'm stumped. Absolutely stumped." Then she laughed, weakly. "Stumped. I made a pun." Not exactly the time for jokes. "Can you find a strong spell? Is there some way you can get me out?"

"I've called Pendress Kennedy. If anyone has the power to reverse this spell, it's her."

I didn't love the idea of Pendress Kennedy being called in to save me. She was the head of my coven, very powerful, and I didn't think she liked me. I hadn't warmed to her either. Still, at this point, I would welcome my worst enemy if they could get me out of here.

I'd never been claustrophobic, but feeling that I was in the middle of a tree trunk was giving me anxiety, especially as the branches were still scraping as they wrapped the cottage tighter and tighter.

Cerridwen was equally unhappy. She kept glaring at me from Lochlan's shoulder.

"Quinn?" The voice sounded far away, but I suspected it was just outside the back door.

"Kathleen?"

"I've got Pendress with me." And then, "What?" she said in a softer voice, as though her head were turned away from me. "Oh, right. Pendress says we should call you. Hang on."

I picked up my cell phone, and it rang. It was Kathleen. "Pendress wants to know exactly what you were doing when you cast the spell."

"It was an accident. I brought home a branch of the yew tree by the graveyard. Everything was fine when I went to bed. This morning, I woke up feeling like I was inside the world's most terrifying treehouse."

I heard a scuffle and then the clear tones of Pendress's voice on the phone. "Quinn, you must be very precise."

"I am. It's exactly like I told Kathleen. I went to bed, and I woke up like this. It must be because I brought home a piece of that yew."

"Foolish thing to have done," she commented. "But that shouldn't have been enough. This is a challenge, even for me."

I didn't like her very much, but I really believed she could help me. "Can you get me out?"

"No. I'll try to find my way in. We might have better luck working at this from the inside out."

"But—" She was already gone.

Lochlan was standing, stroking Cerridwen under the chin, and she finally looked like she was relaxing. Unlike me. He looked at me. "Was that Pendress Kennedy?"

I nodded. "Do you think she can get us out of here?"

"She has great power."

I heard a sound like what I'd experienced driving on the narrowest of Irish roads when the bushes hit the car from either side. And then a thump. It came from the living room. I rushed in, Lochlan right behind me. Pendress was standing there, her hand on Kathleen's wrist. There's an English expression that says she looked like she'd gone through a hedge backward. I now had a perfect visual of what that looked like. Burrs and thorns and bits of greenery covered them both. Pendress's beautiful, flowing hair looked like a bird's nest. And like a perfect little bird's egg, there was a red yew berry hanging precariously. Kathleen was no better. Her glasses hung askew, and her polyester skirt was so badly snagged, I doubted she'd ever be able to wear it again. Not that that was our biggest problem right now.

Pendress let go of Kathleen and said, "Right." Then she noticed Lochlan. "And what's he doing here?"

"He was trying to help," I told them. And before they got any ideas about why a gorgeous dude was in my house so early in the morning, I pointed out the greenery all over his clothes. "He just got here too."

Pendress looked at Lochlan, and her expression was wary, not threatened so much as competitive. Did these two have some rivalry about who was the more powerful of the two? Well, if they worked together and got us out of here, that would be grand, as the Irish liked to say.

Pendress straightened up and ran her hands through her tangled hair. The berry tumbled to the ground. "Right. Now, let's walk you through exactly what you did before you manifested this yew jungle around your cottage."

I didn't think I'd manifested anything. I explained one more time that I'd picked up the yew branch and brought it home, thinking I might fashion a divining rod out of it.

"While I appreciate your attempt to use natural objects and bend them to your will," she said somewhat sarcastically, "perhaps pilfering from one of the most magical trees in Ireland wasn't your best decision." She glared at me. "But I think we can all agree it wasn't your worst."

Ouch. Would I ever live down the way I'd interfered with death? And now that I glanced around with every window and covering thick and black, I felt as though I were personally inside a grave. Worse, I seemed to have brought three magical creatures and a magical cat into my cavern of doom.

Pendress shook herself and mumbled something, and before my eyes she transformed back into her Glinda the Good Witch persona. She didn't bother with poor Kathleen, however, who still looked like she'd lost an argument with a hedge trimmer.

"All right. Walk me through everything you did before this happened."

I wouldn't repeat how I'd gone to bed and woken up in utter darkness. I had made that point. I had to go back. I glanced around the living room and gasped. "Oh."

Everyone followed my startled gaze, and there was that book of shadows sitting in the middle of the table where I'd left it.

Pendress reached it first. She picked it up and opened it. "Where did you get this?" she asked me sharply.

"It was in Billy O'Donnell's books. His daughter, Brenda, dropped them off for me to sell at the shop. It's so old, I thought it must be valuable. So I went to return the book and..." Right. They didn't know about Brenda.

I took a deep breath and quickly told them about Brenda's

death last night. "I brought the old grimoire and a few valuable books home with me for safekeeping."

"So you brought the book of spells here?"

Again with the tone. How was I supposed to know it would cause disaster? "Yes. I brought it here. I didn't know what else to do with it. Lochlan has a friend who's an antiquarian book expert. I was going to ask him if he could value it and then wait until we found out who Brenda O'Donnell's heir is. Or, if it had no value, I would probably just have kept it. It's a beautiful thing. Quite the curiosity."

Pendress was scanning it. "Good goddess. It's more than that. Did you recite any of these spells?"

Kathleen jumped, surprisingly, to my defense. "She couldn't have. Quinn doesn't have the Gaelic."

Pendress kept flipping, and I felt guilty and wretched. And worst of all foolish. In a small voice, I admitted that I had found one spell in middle English. "I only sounded out the words. It didn't occur to me I was casting a spell."

And then they all gave me that look that I dreaded. The one that needs no interpretation. The one that shouts loud and clear, "How could you be so stupid?"

They didn't have to say it aloud, because I was asking it of myself.

"Show me exactly which spell it was." Pendress's silver bracelets tinkled together as she pushed the book at me. "Quickly. The spell is only winding tighter and tighter. If we're ever to get out of here, we must act quickly." As though to underline the urgency, another window broke upstairs.

And that was really helping me focus and find the right page. My hands were trembling so much that finally Lochlan took the book and held it for me. This meant that Cerridwen had to crawl up his chest and hang herself around the back of his neck. Even she, from that position, could glare at me like, if she ever got out of here, she would find a new witch. A familiar was associated with the craft of her witch. If I let her down, I was sure she'd have plenty of better offers.

I didn't want to lose Cerridwen. I didn't want to lose this little cottage. I didn't want to lose this budding new life that I'd just begun to enjoy. I didn't want to die by tree strangulation. I took a deep breath in and forced myself to calm down. And then I tried to block out all the blame coming at me and my natural nervousness of being trapped in this tiny cottage. And then I found it. Almost as though the book had obligingly opened for me to the page I wanted. I passed it to Pendress. Kathleen leaned over her shoulder and read the page too.

Pendress sighed when she finished reading the spell. "Really, Quinn. You should have known better."

I thought that had been made abundantly clear. And underlined.

"Can you reverse it?" Lochlan asked the obvious question.

"We can but try."

Now Pendress was all business. "Quinn, bring out your candles. I will cast a circle." And then we did something I'd never done before. She told me to read the spell over again out loud. My shock must have shown. I didn't say, "Are you crazy?" But I felt it all the same.

"Just do as I tell you," she snapped. "I'll explain later."

I looked at the window, even blacker if possible than the last time I'd looked. The yew was wrapping itself tighter and tighter around the cottage. The air smelled like a forest and damp earth. Every minute counted. I nodded. Kathleen arranged and lit candles, Pendress cast the circle, and at her signal, I began to read the words of the spell. Honestly, I felt like I was reading my death sentence. My voice was low, and I stumbled over the unfamiliar words.

I barely got to the end of the first line when Pendress spoke over me. I tried to ignore her musical voice so I could concentrate on the words I was reading, but she was doing something I'd never seen done before. She was reversing the spell while I was reading it. I got through, and I had the sense that maybe the atmosphere was lightening. But I didn't dare even look up from the page. "Again," Pendress directed. I doggedly read on. And Pendress's voice continued. I thought she was speaking in Gaelic.

I got to the end, and then she took the book from my hands and put it in the middle of the circle, and we three witches held hands.

Already daylight was coming through the remaining branches. And they were falling away with every second. We stood there, hands clasped. Pendress said,

Here we stand, we magic three
From this circle of safety we ask of thee
To free us from this cursed tree
As we will, so mote it be

The candles flickered, and sunlight began to enter the room as the branches fell until the windows were clear, and then Pendress nodded. We broke contact, and with a flick of her wrist, she blew out the candles and closed the circle.

Lochlan hadn't been part of the circle, obviously, but he'd observed. "That was quite impressive," he said.

Pendress gave a superior smirk. I wondered how much

extra pizzazz and showmanship she'd added to the ritual for his benefit.

I didn't care. She'd managed it; that was all that mattered. I was puzzled though. As I'd recited the words again, I'd made some sense of them. "That wasn't a curse aimed at wrapping a house in foliage," I said. "It sounded to me like a spell for bringing a loved one closer."

"Between having a piece of that yew inside your cottage and reading anything in that book of shadows, you opened the way for that old witch's energy to enter this house."

"So I could have read anything in there and the effect would have been the same?"

"Even opening the covers was dangerous. Like the lid of Pandora's box."

I eyed the ancient book the way I'd watch a venomous snake that had me in its sights. "What do I do with the book?"

"I'll take it away with me. I have a special library. It will be safe."

I didn't know what to do. I glanced at Kathleen, who nodded.

"And there's a fire pit out back," I told them. "I'm going to take that yew branch and burn it."

Again, Pendress shook her head. "That tree branch has wonderful power. I'll take that with me as well and keep it safe."

I was getting a grim feeling about this. If this woman kept taking everything that had dark power attached to it, what would that make her capable of?

Kathleen looked like she might say something but then pressed her lips together as though not daring. I couldn't help recalling that Lucinda had told me she'd made a powerful enemy, and that's why she had to leave here. Could that enemy be Pendress Kennedy? And was that Glinda the Good Witch thing a complete act?

Pendress picked up the ancient book of spells, and as she did so, the book glowed a peculiar color of blue. No one seemed to notice but me and Cerridwen, who stared at me intently. Going on nothing but instinct, I said, "No."

CHAPTER 8

*E*veryone turned to look at me because I'd said the word in a firm voice that didn't sound like mine. I looked at the head of my coven, determined to hold my ground. "No. You cannot take that book of spells. It doesn't belong to you, and it doesn't belong to me. Brenda gave it to me for safekeeping and now she's dead. I need to give the grimoire to her heirs, whoever they are."

Pendress looked astonished that I'd given her the grimoire and then taken it back again. "You would give this book to a human? When you know what it's capable of?"

"Pendress, I'm not a newly fledged witch. In all my years practicing the craft, I have never witnessed anything like what happened. Instead of rushing away with the book and that yew branch, why don't you tell me what's going on?"

She tapped her silver-polished fingernails on the cover of the book. She looked at Kathleen, who shrugged and nodded. "Very well. You're involved anyway. You're part of it."

"Part of what?"

"I'm not entirely sure. But I suspect that this is the missing book of Biddy O'Donnell."

"Who was Biddy O'Donnell?" I had to ask. "And was she anything to do with Billy and Brenda O'Donnell?" Seemed like a reasonable question, seeing they'd owned the book.

She walked to the window and stared out at the choppy sea. It was astonishing to see the sunshine dancing off the waves when it had been so terrifyingly dark in here not so very long ago. "Biddy O'Donnell was a renowned witch. Powerful."

"But if her magic was so powerful, and her book is so powerful, why have we seen nothing like this before? Surely there would have been stories of peculiar happenings in and around Ballydehag."

"Because her grimoire has been gathering dust in the home of a man who had no magic. When you recited that spell, you with your magic, you released something dangerous. And then, add in the branch from that ancient and magical yew tree, and you increased the power of the spell by something like tenfold."

I was surprised. "The yew tree is that powerful?"

She gave me a thin smile. "That tree has kept evil tamped down for four hundred years. Trimming it was like giving Samson a crewcut."

I looked at the branch. It seemed so innocuous.

"The tree's lost much of its power to hold in the dangerous evil that lives beneath its roots. But also the tree has drawn up the nutrients from the soil for all these hundreds of years. Naturally, it's also drawn up negative energy. So, when you cast that spell, even though you didn't realize you were doing it, in the presence of a recently cut branch of the yew tree, well, you saw what happened."

"And yet you were able to reverse that spell. How did you know how to do it?"

I remembered the sound of our two voices mingling and weaving in amongst each other's—her melodious voice rising and falling as she intoned the words of her spell, my halting attempts to read Middle English, stumbling over the unfamiliar phrases—but still I had felt our words weaving together as though we were binding together a rope.

There was silence. Cerridwen came over and rubbed against my legs until I picked her up. Finally, Pendress said, "I recognized this book. You see, Biddy O'Donnell was kin to one of my ancestors."

I knew Ireland was old and its magic was ancient, but this was really something. "Your ancestor was a witch?"

"She was."

"Do you have her book?"

"I do."

Kathleen and she shared a glance that seemed full of meaning, which I couldn't interpret. Kathleen said, "You'll have to tell her."

Cerridwen rubbed her head beneath my chin, and I felt comforted. Whatever happened, she and I were at least together.

I didn't like the expression on Pendress's face. That Madonna-like serenity was at odds with the eyes that were as sharp as ice picks. "Did you think it was coincidence that brought you back here, Quinn? Of all the places we could have sent you, did you not wonder why we brought you back to Ireland?"

"Back to Ireland? I've never been here."

"Your kin have."

"But my family came from Ireland about three generations ago. I don't have any connection with Ireland."

"Foolish witch. Of course, you do. Trace back your lineage, and you will discover Biddy O'Donnell was your direct ancestor. Your magic flows directly through the female line from her."

I stared at the grimoire in her arms. "My ancestor was the kind of witch who traps people in their houses with thorns?" Not to mention she'd been executed for supposedly horrible crimes, though I was reserving judgment on that. Still, it was like finding out your great-granny was a famous serial killer. Not exactly the best news.

"She was. And, for reasons I don't yet understand, your destiny is here."

"So you didn't just randomly pick up a pawn, me, from the edge of your chessboard, all the way out in Seattle, and plonk me here in the middle of Ireland for no reason."

"Oh, there was every reason."

My heart was thudding, and even Cerridwen was stiff and alert in my arms. "What else have you been keeping from me?" Because I could sense there was more.

They both looked at Lochlan, who'd been silently watching our little melodrama unfold. "He's not one of us. He has no place here," Pendress said.

I didn't know Lochlan all that well, but he'd been the first one to notice my distress, and he'd torn through thick thorns and branches to get to me. I wasn't about to kick him out. I said, again finding a firmness that surprised me when facing this somewhat terrifying witch, "He's part of this. He stays."

When she shrugged her shoulders, the crystals at her neck sparkled. "Then let it be your responsibility."

I nodded.

Pendress said, "They buried Biddy O'Donnell under the yew tree where she's remained for four hundred years. When she died, she swore vengeance and that she would be back."

This Biddy O'Donnell didn't sound like a very nice gal. "You're certain she was a witch?"

Pendress offered me the grimoire as proof.

"Was she a black witch?"

"Black is so definitive. I prefer the term dark."

You say tomato and I say tomahto.

I was having trouble taking this in. "You're saying that I am directly descended from a dark witch who's been buried here in Ballydehag for centuries? A woman so powerful she needed a magic tree to keep her underground?"

"How do you think you got the power to cheat death?"

The area around my heart felt cold all of a sudden, as though it had been wrapped in ice. "I've always tried to follow the rules and do the right thing. I thought I was a white witch." My voice was rising, and I swallowed, trying to control myself.

"We see that. A witch isn't dark or white purely by destiny. Witches choose how they use their power."

Well, that was a relief, anyway. However, she continued, "But when you chose to use that very powerful spell that you knew was wrong, to pull your husband back to the living when he'd already begun his passage, you knew you were toying with the dark arts."

The cold feeling around my heart was spreading to the rest of me. She was right. I had known. "Are you saying I'm a dark witch who's been masquerading as a white one all these years?"

It was like finding out I was evil when all my life I'd counted myself one of the good guys.

"I'm only saying that you have to be very careful. We all choose how we use our powers. But most of us don't have the power that you have. Your lineage is strong and contains as many famously good witches as famously bad ones."

Was that supposed to make me feel better? "Did you bring me here to keep an eye on me?"

They both shook their heads in unison. "The prophecy seems to be coming true. We think Biddy O'Donnell may rise again."

"What!" I shrieked the word. Cerridwen was so unnerved, she jumped out of my arms and ran to the corner, staring at me with wide eyes. I'd have comforted her except that I felt wide-eyed with fright myself. I wouldn't have blamed her if she ran as far away from me as she could get. A familiar was intimately bound with its witch. She must be regretting the terrible mistake she'd made.

I was thinking wild thoughts. Just by reading a spell I didn't understand, I'd wound this cottage in almost impenetrable branches and thorns. But if it weren't for that broken piece of yew, I bet that spell wouldn't have done anything particularly serious. Especially as I didn't understand what I was saying. Pendress was just scaremongering. I wasn't sure whether she was really after my apparently many, many times distant grandmother or whether she was trying to frighten me into obedience. I said, "If it hadn't been for that yew being pruned, I don't think the spell would have had this power."

Pendress's eyes flashed. "And do you think it's a coincidence, Quinn? That that yew, which has held that witch in place, has suddenly lost so much of its power?"

"Of course, it's a coincidence. Father O'Flanagan said that tree was interfering with the graveyard. He hired tree surgeons from Cork City. Yes, it's a coincidence."

She shook her head. And, like an echo, Kathleen shook hers. "It's the witch's doing. She must have a creature aboveground who is serving her."

"Not poor Father O'Flanagan. He's a Catholic priest."

She shook her head again. "No. It's not the father. He's merely a pawn."

I knew how the poor man felt. We were all pieces on this board, and I did not understand whose was the guiding hand. Or how this game would end.

A terrible thought occurred to me. That face in the mirror at Brenda O'Donnell's house that only I'd seen. That message scrawled on the mirror.

I had a horrible feeling that Biddy O'Donnell might already be back.

CHAPTER 9

I looked outside, and I could see sunshine, and the atmosphere in here was still dark and ominous even though the windows were now clear. I suddenly felt claustrophobic and needed to get outside. "Why don't we get outside and get some air."

"If you wish."

She walked toward the front door, and I stopped her. "Pendress. The grimoire."

She hesitated and then put the old, leather-covered book down on the table. "Remember, Quinn, this is a book of enormous power. It belongs to you, so I must respect your wishes, but you must be very, very careful with it."

Laying aside the drama melting from her words, did she not think I'd figured that out by now?

I merely nodded.

And we all walked outside into the sunshine. I lifted my face up to feel the warmth of the sun's rays. There had been some bad moments back there when I'd wondered if I'd ever breathe fresh air or feel the sun on my face again. I turned to look at my cottage, and it was as though the building had never been touched. The climbing roses bloomed as brightly, their leaves a glossy green against the white cottage walls. I'd heard glass breaking, but no windows appeared damaged. They sparkled as though newly washed. I went closer to the roses, and their scent seemed even sweeter than usual.

I'd expected the garden would look like a forest after a terrible storm, but there wasn't so much as a yew needle on the ground. The entire incident could have been a dream.

Lochlan said, "I'm glad you're all right, Quinn. I'll leave you three now."

He didn't exactly shrink from the sun, but he wasn't shoving his face in it like I was. I followed him into the shadows beneath an apple tree. "Thank you."

He looked over at the two witches talking intently to each other and then back at me. "I'm always here if you need me. Be careful."

I shuddered at his words. "Believe me, I will."

With a curt nod of his head, he turned and strode away back toward his lonely castle, Devil's Keep. I wondered if my ancestor had once owned it. It seemed like the sort of place Biddy O'Donnell would call home.

I watched his tall figure retreat, and then I turned back toward the two witches swapping secrets on my front lawn. I didn't have to be a witch to know that they were gossiping about me.

I walked up to them and interrupted. "If this Biddy O'Donnell has someone above ground doing her bidding, we have to find them."

"Yes," Pendress said.

"Could they have caused Brenda's death?"

Kathleen looked to Pendress for an answer. She said, "I don't know. I can't see it. I believe it's possible. If Biddy O'Donnell has an agent here, she may have been desperate to get her hands on the book and, believing Brenda O'Donnell had the grimoire but unable to find it, could have lashed out in a rage."

Not how anybody wanted to go. And why did I feel guilty? Like this was my fault? Was I responsible for the actions of some ancient ancestor of mine?

Still, her blood, and presumably her magic, ran in my veins. I felt like getting an emergency blood transfusion.

"There's something else you should know."

Pendress put a hand to her heart. "I'm not sure I can sustain more revelations."

She wasn't going to like this one. "I've seen a... presence in the O'Donnell house."

Kathleen looked like she'd swallowed a spider. "You said so during Billy O'Donnell's wake, but I thought it was only Billy not quite passed over."

"I don't think it was Billy," I said.

Pendress was looking at me, and her eyes were as clear and cool as a bottomless lake. "What exactly happened?"

"At Billy's wake, I felt strange. Like there was something heavy and dark in the house. I went upstairs to the bathroom, and this terrifying face was looking back at me from the mirror."

"What did it look like?"

How to describe it? "Female. Old and shriveled with angry, dark eyes."

"And it was looking at you from the mirror?"

"Yes. And last night, Brenda was hurt and asked me for water. I went into the bathroom, and there was writing on the mirror. It was in red. I thought it was blood, but it could have been lipstick. The message read, "Go away, you're not wanted here.""

"Rather childish, don't you think?" Pendress sounded mildly amused while I still felt a clutch of dread at my throat. And yet, when I stepped past my fear, I could see her point.

"You think it's a coincidence that message was on the mirror the night Brenda died?"

"I don't know. What happened to the message?"

One thing I really admired about Pendress was that she often asked exactly the right question. "It disappeared. I was going to show the police, but it was gone when I went back."

"Which makes me think the message was for you, not Brenda."

"But while Brenda was dying? Why leave it then?"

Pendress stared at the roses as though they might answer. The way my day was going so far, I wouldn't have been a bit surprised if they had. However, the flowers remained mute. Finally, Pendress said, "Perhaps the ghost, for want of a better term, is sending you messages, so the fact that you were there is what caused the writing to appear on the mirror."

"And Brenda's death was unconnected to the writing on the mirror?" I asked.

"That depends on who killed Brenda."

And we were back to that. "I need to find out what happened to her." Brenda had only come to Ballydehag to bury her father. She'd been on her way back to Dublin, and her life, when it was so cruelly taken away from her. I said what I was thinking. "Why would an ancient witch, or her minion, have killed Brenda? What did they stand to gain?"

"I have no idea. I agree, it's not logical, but anger and disappointment make witches do foolish things." Pendress reminded me.

I wasn't convinced. I had a pretty good radar, and I hadn't sensed any other witches but Kathleen in the area. And Pendress when she chose to show up. Coincidences happened. I wondered if Brenda's death might in fact be nothing to do with supernatural powers but have a very human cause.

"I think I'll do a bit of digging and see what I can uncover about Brenda and her past. What if a human committed her murder? Someone with very human motives?"

"That's an excellent idea," Pendress said to my surprise. "Rule out the human element. And then we'll look to see whether magic may have played a role. If Biddy O'Donnell is causing trouble from the grave, we must stop her."

We all agreed and went our separate ways.

I glanced back at my cottage. I didn't want to go into it. What if it got wrapped in greenery again? And had I done a really stupid thing in hanging on to that book of shadows? I should have let Pendress take it when she'd wanted to. Just get it out of here. But my instinct had been so strong when I'd seen the blue light around that book as she'd touched it. I hadn't made it to this age without understanding that I needed to listen to my instincts.

I had to do something. I couldn't stand all the frustrated energy that was coursing through me. I wanted to find out who had killed Brenda and why. And please let it be nothing to do with me or any ancestor I possessed, or any curse-laden grimoire that may have accidently come into my hands. I didn't want to think that Brenda had been killed by a surprised burglar or a random murderer, but I preferred both those theories to one where I or my family were somehow involved. And as for that yew tree, I would go up there right now, and if those tree surgeons were at work, I'd make them stop. I'd put a spell on them if I had to.

Now that I had a purpose, I grabbed the bicycle that was leaning against the side of my shed. I was too wired to drive. The exercise would do me good. I got on the bike and began to pedal. At least this dispelled some of my crazy energy. I rode through town and then turned onto the road that led to the church. I was going so fast that when I turned down the lane to see if the tree surgeons were still at work, I took the curve much too wide and all but collided with a dusty van coming toward me.

I hit my brakes hard and turned the front wheel, not even thinking, just acting on instinct. I spewed gravel, and the bike, meant for meandering down country lanes, not the Tour de France, skidded out from under me. I felt myself fly through the air and landed on my back in the middle of the lane. I felt the impact and wondered for a second if I might be dead. I couldn't breathe.

The dusty van that had nearly hit me also came to a gravel-spewing halt. I heard the engine stall, and then while I tried to get my breath back, heard the door open and slam. Footsteps approached. If I could just take a breath, I might manage to get up. I didn't want to lie here in the gravel while some stranger came upon me.

The footsteps stopped. I was conscious of a figure bending, and then into my line of vision came the very concerned face of Dr. Andrew Milsom, or Drew as he insisted I call him. Instead of saying what any other person would have said—which was "Are you all right?"—he said, "Lie still." Very bossy. Still, I had no choice. I couldn't get my lungs to work. I just lay there as he'd told me to.

"Why aren't you wearing a helmet?" he said, sounding very annoyed.

There hadn't been a helmet in the shed. But I could see now that I'd been pretty stupid not to wear one. He ran his hands over me very professionally. Finally, I could take a breath. It was short and sharp, but at least I got some air into my lungs. "I'm okay," I gasped.

"I'll be the judge of that."

"Who do you think you are, God?"

I felt irritable and manhandled. And really humiliated to be lying on my back in the middle of a gravel road.

"Not God, but close. The only doctor in Ballydehag. You want to stay on my good side."

The words were sort of humorous, but his expression anything but. Finally, he seemed satisfied. "You've not broken anything. Did you hit your head?"

"How am I supposed to remember? I fell off my bike." How humiliating. I hadn't done that since I was about ten years old.

He helped me to my feet. And stood ready in case I collapsed. Which I didn't. I pulled up the sleeve of my sweater, and my elbow was bleeding. My palm was cut and had small pieces of gravel embedded in it. And my hip and knee were sore. But other than that, I thought I'd got off pretty lightly.

He took my hand in his and turned it palm up. "Come on back to the surgery. I'll get that cleaned up."

I wanted to tell him I could take care of it myself. I had a salve and some spells. But freaking out the doctor, and as he'd so rightly pointed out, the only doctor in town, was probably not a great idea. Without me even answering him, he picked up my bike and put it in the back of the van.

He took my arm, even though I didn't ask him to, and helped me to the passenger-side door. Probably just as well, because when I tried to walk, my knee threatened to give way. Still, I sucked it up and managed to get myself into the passenger seat of the van. He walked around and got back into the driver's side and turned around and headed back toward his home, where he had his surgery.

"How did you come to be driving like a bat out of hell? And on the wrong side of the road?"

"Bat out of hell is a bit strong, don't you think? That old bike only has one speed. Besides, I'm American. I keep getting confused about which is the correct side of the road."

"Well, until you get it right, I strongly recommend that you slow down."

"Good advice."

He turned and shot me a sharp glance. "And get yourself a helmet."

I rolled my eyes. "Yes, Dad."

"Dad? You really think I'm old enough to be your father?" He sounded so shocked that I suspected what he wanted to say was, have a look in the mirror.

He pulled up to his surgery, and by this time, my knee was really stiffening up. He had to help me out of the van, and I hopped. Luckily, it wasn't too far. He helped me inside, and I was glad that his surgery was closed at the moment so there were only the two of us in it, and I didn't have an audience to witness me bashed up and humiliated.

It was also his day off. "I'm really sorry to trouble you in your time off," I said.

"And so you should be. I'll expect all the newest fishing books published as payment."

Was he joking? The trouble with Andrew Milsom was it was difficult to tell. He had that wry English humor that I didn't entirely get.

"Can you get up on the examining table? Or do you need a hand?"

"I can do it." Still, it was a struggle.

"I'd insist on the hospital, but I think you've merely wrenched your knee, and I can take care of that hand quite quickly. However, if the pain doesn't go away or the limp gets worse, you'll have to go to the A and E."

"A and E?"

"What you'd call the emergency room."

"Where is it?" I hadn't seen a hospital anywhere near here.

"In Cork city. That's the closest." It was where Brenda had been taken only last night.

I was sure I'd be fine. Still, before he even troubled with my hand, he opened my eyes and shone a light in them. I knew he was checking me for concussion. "I didn't hit my head," I reminded him.

"It's very easy to hit your head and not remember it. Especially if you have a concussion."

When he'd satisfied himself that I didn't have a concussion, Drew cleaned up my hand and elbow for me. He was gentle and quick. I felt awful, though, because he was dressed for the outdoors. I didn't think he got a lot of time off. "What am I taking you from?"

"Fishing."

"Of course. I should have realized." The only time he'd been in my shop, it had been to pick up a fishing book he'd ordered. "Is that why you moved here?" I was curious why anyone who hadn't grown up in this small village even discovered it, never mind decided to make it their home. Unless, like me, you'd been essentially banished here.

"That's right. I came up here on a fishing trip a few years ago and always thought I'd come back. Maybe retire here. It happened a little quicker than I thought."

There was clearly a story here, but he didn't seem in a hurry to tell me more, and I didn't pry. I wondered if Karen's gossip had been correct and he'd left London because of a cheating wife and best friend. He dabbed a final disinfectant cream on the heel of my hand where the scraping was the worst. "There's not much point bandaging it. Try and keep it clean."

He wrote me out a prescription. "This is for anti-inflammatory pills for your knee and hip. The chemist in town will carry the drugs."

I nodded. "I feel terrible that I interrupted your fishing."

"You didn't, really. I'll drop you and your bike back at your cottage, and then I'll be on my way. I'm only an hour later than I'd hoped to be. The fish will wait."

It was a little embarrassing how much he had to help me get back to his van and hoist myself up again into the passenger seat. I'd stiffened up even more just in the brief time I'd been in his surgery. "I really should have examined that leg."

I shook my head. It would have been so weird. I was wearing jeans, and he'd have had to find me a gown, and I think both of us felt a little awkward. It would be different if his nurse was sitting out front, and the surgery was open, but being here off hours, I really didn't feel like taking my pants off in front of the only single man in town who was around my age.

It flashed across my mind that at some point I would have to have my lady parts checked. A Pap test and so on. I needed to find a female doctor in a nearby town.

"Where were you going to in such a hurry, anyway?" he asked me as we drove slowly back to my cottage.

It was Saturday. I'd wanted to stop the tree surgeons before I opened the shop at ten. If I hadn't been so freaked out, I'd have realized that tree surgeons probably didn't work on a Saturday. However, I'd also needed to get rid of some of the adrenaline coursing through me since nearly being squeezed to death by tree branches and finding out an ancestor of mine might have been involved in Brenda O'Donnell's murder.

I went with part of the truth. "I'm pretty upset about Brenda."

He nodded. "I'm sorry you had to see her like that."

"Me, too. But at least she had someone with her. Archie was completely freaked out when I got there."

He shot me a sideways glance. "Archie's a nice lad but not one you want to rely on in an emergency. I'm glad you were with her too."

"Mostly I held her hand and talked to her. I kept assuring

her that help was on its way and she'd feel better soon. Just babbling. I felt so helpless."

"No. It was the right thing to do. To let her know she was safe."

"Did she say anything to you?"

He sent me a curious look as though he was rethinking his diagnosis about the concussion. "Brenda O'Donnell?"

"Yes. She asked me for some water, but by the time I got it for her, she'd lost consciousness. I wonder if she said anything on her way to the hospital."

He swerved to miss a pothole, and it seemed to take all his attention. Then, with a tiny shake of his head, as though he knew he were breaking the rules by telling me, he admitted, "She said, 'Our Father.' "

I turned to look at him, and even moving my head hurt. I took care not to wince, though, or he'd have me in the hospital having a CAT scan. I was certain I'd only had the wind knocked out of me, but every muscle in my body was seizing up. I needed a very hot bath and some of my potent herbs. And I needed them soon. Much as I appreciated the muscle relaxants, I'd use my own remedies.

I needed to stop thinking about my own aches and pains and focus. When was I going to get another chance to interview Andrew Milsom? "Our Father. That's all she said?"

"It is."

"What do you think it meant?"

He glanced over at me. "The woman was near death. We're in Ireland. I think it meant she wanted a priest to administer her last rites."

Brenda had seemed a very modern Irish woman. I wasn't

entirely certain that I agreed with him. However, I was curious. "So did she get them?"

He nodded. "We managed it, in the nick of time. We couldn't save her life, but at least she was given last rites by a priest."

"Our Father," I said again softly, almost to myself.

"I wish I could have saved her. She seemed like a nice woman."

I nodded. "Too nice to kill."

CHAPTER 10

*T*uesday, I was working in the shop when an older woman came in. It took me a second to recognize her as Brenda's former teacher, Bridget Sullivan. She didn't even pretend she was here to look at books. She came straight up to me and took my hand. "I heard that you were the one that found our poor Brenda."

She seemed so much older than the last time I'd seen her. "It was Archie Mahoney who discovered her, but I was there soon after. Would you like to sit down?" I gestured to the pair of overstuffed, chintz chairs where I'd given Brenda tea only a few days earlier. She nodded and sat down. "I don't know why I came to you. I wanted... I need to understand what happened."

I understood how she felt. "All I can tell you is what I found. Do you really want to hear it?"

"No, I don't want to. But I feel I should. I can't stop thinking about poor Brenda."

There was someone waiting at the till to pay, so I asked her to wait a moment. I took care of my customer and then put the "back in ten minutes" sign on the door. I put the kettle on and brewed a cup of tea. If I'd ever seen anyone who needed a cup of calming tea, it was Bridget Sullivan.

"Thank you, dear," she said, then she sipped and sat back and seemed to gather her forces together. "Tell me what you found."

I respected this woman too much to lie to her, but I could honestly say that I didn't think Brenda had suffered. I told her she'd asked me for water when I got there and that she'd seemed to fall asleep. And then Andrew Milsom had gone with her in the ambulance to the hospital.

She nodded. "That's good. I'm glad she wasn't alone at the end. She had people who cared about her."

"Yes, she did."

I asked Bridget Sullivan what I'd been asking myself over and over. "But who would do such a thing?"

She looked at me with her sharp, old eyes and then dropped her gaze back down to her tea. I was transported back to the argument I'd witnessed at Billy O'Donnell's wake. "I saw you with Brenda and a man at the wake. They were arguing, and you broke it up. You told him he couldn't come inside the house. I didn't overhear everything, but I'm sure he told you that Brenda had ruined his life."

Her laugh sounded bitter and rusty. "The boot was on the other foot. Jack Buckley was one of those boys who seemed they could do anything they turned their mind to. He was always beautiful and engaging and cheeky, and he used to get away with murder. Brenda was studious. One of the brightest minds I ever had the pleasure of teaching. And she loved to learn. But when a girl gets to a certain age, she enters a period where scholarship isn't the most important thing on her mind. No doubt you know exactly what I mean."

I'd been a teenager. Naturally, I knew. "So, Brenda and Jack?"

She nodded. "Inseparable they were. I didn't like it. I didn't think he was a good influence on her. But he was a charmer, and she was quite willing to be charmed."

"What happened?"

She put her hand to her forehead as though it was paining her. "If that poor girl weren't lying dead, I would never tell you what I am about to share. And even though she is, I ask that you keep this confidential. It all happened a long time ago, and she became a wonderful, strong woman. That's the person we must remember."

"Of course."

"Drugs. That's what happened."

I'd thought of ways that a naïve girl who was too smart for her own good could get in trouble with a swaggering smoothie like Jack, and drugs were not the first thing that had leapt to my mind. I felt my eyes open wide. "Drugs? Really?"

"I know. Astonishing, isn't it? It happens in the best families. I can tell you as a former teacher, it happens in all families. But it was Jack who got her into the drugs. Her marks went down. Her attitude changed. She began missing school, something that was unheard of for her. She denied that she was taking drugs, but I'd been around too long to be fooled."

I so felt for her. I could imagine a dedicated teacher with one of her brightest students going off the rails like that and how helpless she'd feel. And how enraged. "What did you do?"

"I went to her father. He was furious and heartbroken and

tried various forms of punishment, none of which worked. I went to Jack's parents. By that time, he'd already left school. They were unable or unwilling to help. Lord knows how long it would have continued or how it would have ended, except Jack was arrested."

"Arrested for drug trafficking?"

She shook her head. "For manslaughter."

The hairs on the back of my neck stood, as though someone had blown chilly air. "Jack killed someone?"

"Had a fight with his dealer, didn't he? They were both high as kites. But the man died. And Jack went to jail."

"And then Brenda saw that he was bad news and cleaned up?"

She shook her head. "I wish she had. But Brenda stood by him. He swore up and down that he was innocent. He hadn't killed the man. Somebody else had. And Brenda believed him. He could have said the sun was black and she'd have believed that too. In fact, for her, I think the sun did turn black when they took him away.

"I was beside myself. There was a slim chance that we could help her turn her life around, but how? Perhaps I was a bit devious. But I said to her the best way she could help Jack was to go to university and study to become a lawyer. She could take his case, prove him innocent and get him out of jail. I told her stories of convicted criminals being set free years later."

"That was smart of you."

She sipped tea. "It fired her imagination. She saw herself as a heroine rescuing the love of her life and exonerating an innocent man. We were nearly too late, however. Her grades had slipped so badly. But she was brilliant, she was tenacious, and I've never seen anyone work so hard as she did. She got into Cork University. She had to get herself off the drugs first. And that's not an easy feat. Not for anyone. But that girl has grit and determination. And she did it. And she got on so brilliantly that she ended up at Trinity College." Bridget sounded as proud as though Brenda had been her own child.

"And did she plead his case and get him out of jail?"

The old teacher shook her head. "She reviewed the evidence and didn't believe him. No. She didn't get him out. And he never forgave her for it. Eight years he spent in prison. And he blames her. Not himself for his foolish choices and his bad temper. He blamed that beautiful woman."

"Did he blame her enough to kill her?"

Those faded but still sharp eyes were stern. "Who else would want to kill her?"

"Have you told the police all this?"

"Of course, I have. He has an alibi." She sounded very disappointed, and I didn't blame her.

"What is it?"

"Archie Mahoney. He was helping Brenda pack up the house, and she sent him off for a dinner break. Jack says Archie came to pick up a distributor cap for that old car of his. Jack works in Ballydehag Motors, you see. Then he went to his niece's birthday party. A dozen people confirm he was there."

Bridget Sullivan might be disappointed not to be able to pin this on Jack, but she wasn't the only one. If the most likely culprit hadn't killed Brenda, then I was more and more worried that my long-departed and not at all missed ancestor could be to blame.

TUESDAY NIGHT, I pounded up the stairs to the upper room of my shop, feeling like I was going to explode. I could hear the conversation going. How could they sound so calm? How could anyone be calm when the world was so crazy?

I burst in on the conversation. Vaguely I heard them talking about Sir Arthur Conan Doyle. Right, that was the book we were discussing this week.

Lady Cork was saying, "Rache, revenge is always a reliable motive for murder, but would one really allow oneself to be so consumed with revenge as to wait decades to kill?"

And then when she saw me, her words petered out. "Quinn, whatever ails you? You look quite wild."

Wild was exactly how I felt. "I'm sorry to interrupt, but I didn't know where to go. I need to talk something through, and I want some honest responses."

They all perked up then. I got the feeling that they may have discussed A Study in Scarlet before, possibly several times, and they were happy for a diversion. Before I could launch into my problems, Lochlan Balfour came toward me. He locked his gaze with mine, and somehow those cool, blue eyes calmed me down a little bit. Perhaps because his own heart beat so very slowly, mine began to regulate too. He watched me for probably a minute and then nodded slowly. "That's better. Come and sit down. May I get you something?"

I realized now how parched I was. "Water?"

He didn't exactly snap his fingers, but he made a gesture, and a young vampire immediately went running down the stairs. He returned with a cool glass of water, which I drank thirstily. I had all their attention now, and I didn't know how to begin. The beginning, like every good book, that was the place to begin.

"As you all know, Brenda O'Donnell was murdered."

Everyone nodded.

"No, that's not it. I have to go back. I got this book. A grimoire. It had belonged to Brenda, or Brenda's father, I should say. It's a book of spells. But it's very old and in sounding out the words of one of them, I accidentally ..." I couldn't even go into how I'd been wrapped in branches and thorns in my own cottage. It was too much. I was trying to forget it. I continued, "It turns out that the book belonged to Biddy O'Donnell."

Now I really had their attention. "Biddy O'Donnell? The one who's buried under the yew tree?" Lady Cork turned to Lochlan. "I wasn't here then, but you were. Didn't they bury her upside down?"

"They did. And laid a very heavy stone over the top of her. And the tree was meant to keep her down. But some fool, namely Father O'Flanagan, decided the tree needed pruning."

Lady Cork shook her head. "Oh, that's bad. I remember the stories."

I put the empty water glass down on my desk. "Well, it turns out that I'm related to Biddy O'Donnell."

Oscar Wilde look fascinated. "So you really are an evil little witch," he said, looking rather amused.

"Well, I'm certainly related to one." Though I knew I had some dark magic in me. I suspected every witch did. That didn't mean I was dark, did it? Or that everything I touched, no matter my intention, went wrong? I felt like I wasn't cursed with dark magic so much as I was cursed with bad luck.

"Anyway, I feel like it's my fault. Somehow, me getting hold of that grimoire and reading that spell aloud in combination with the pruning of that tree has freed Biddy O'Donnell." I glanced around, and my calmness deserted me once again. "I'm afraid that it's my fault Brenda's dead. I didn't kill her, but I might as well have picked up that heavy candlestick and bludgeoned her myself."

The line didn't have as dramatic an effect as it probably would have if I were in regular, human company. To a bunch of vampires who had been around a long time, I supposed a bit of bludgeoning wasn't anything to get too excited about.

"You know what our good friend Conan Doyle says," Oscar Wilde drawled. "Once you eliminate the impossible, whatever remains, no matter how improbable, must be the truth." He tossed his head so his hair shifted on his shoulders. "Of course, in our case, we must reverse the aphorism. When we eliminate the plausible, what remains must be magic."

I hung onto his words like a dog waiting for a liver treat. Honestly, I was practically salivating at the idea that he might have some theory that would mean I wasn't responsible for another woman's death.

He had the floor now, which he always preferred. He rose. Tonight he was wearing an evening cloak, black and silk-lined. There was a top hat on the chair beside him. Oscar liked to dress for book club. He picked up his silver-headed walking cane, not that he had any trouble walking, but it was another affectation. And it made a very good pointer. He waved it in the air. "Let us put aside for the moment the idea that a supernatural curse is responsible for this woman's death. And let us look at other possibilities."

I wanted to cling to his theory. I was ready to throw myself on the ground and wrap my arms around his ankles and let him drag me around with him as he paced up and down. But I didn't want to ruin his concentration. "Take that away, and who else might have wanted that woman dead?"

Everyone looked at me. I shrugged. "I don't know. I'm just getting to know the place myself."

"Aye. That's probably excellent," said Deirdre, in her Scottish accent. She'd abandoned her Chanel suit this week and was wearing a turquoise knit dress. "It means you have a fresh eye."

"It also means I don't know who might have wanted her dead. She grew up here, I know that, and then went away for college and never came home."

"Then we must find out more about her. Do you have any idea who might have done it, Quinn?" This was Lochlan. I could always rely on him to be analytical and precise.

"Yes. There's a man called Jack." And I told them how he and Brenda had been a crazy hot item when they were teenagers and how he'd got her into drugs and then got himself in huge trouble by killing, either accidentally or on purpose, a drug dealer.

"Well, that sounds like an open and shut case to me," Oscar said. "Drugs, eh? Our old friend Conan Doyle knew something about that."

"I wish it was that simple. But the person who told me about him also said he had an alibi for the night she was killed." I told them about Archie going in for a distributor cap and then Jack heading for his niece's birthday party.

Bartholomew Branson, the thriller writer who hadn't been a vampire for very long, jumped to his feet. "Okay," he said. "We can help Quinn. Find out if the guy's alibi holds." He glanced around. "Who's with me?"

Oops. Bartholomew's disappearance was still news. Not hot news anymore, since he'd disappeared from a cruise ship a couple of months ago now and no sign of him had been found. It was generally accepted that he'd fallen overboard and drowned. Still, he couldn't go wandering around Ireland without someone recognizing him.

"I've got contacts in the Guards," Lochlan said in a cool, soothing tone. "I'll see what I can find out."

These vamps had contacts everywhere. Were there actually vampires working for the Irish police force? Or were they just friendly with Lochlan, not knowing who he really was? I probably didn't need to know the answer. In fact, it was probably best if I didn't pry.

"While you're at it, can you get a copy of the post-mortem?"

He nodded, slowly. "Any particular reason why?"

"No. I'm grasping at straws. I want to make absolutely certain that it was that head wound that killed her."

"I'll find out for you."

I felt better just feeling like the vampires were on my side. Yes, I had witches I could turn to, but the trouble with witches was that they were much less likely than the vampires to believe it was a human that had killed Brenda O'Donnell. They were all absolutely convinced it was a combination of me arriving in this place where I apparently had history, Father O'Flanagan getting that tree pruned, and Biddy O'Donnell taking advantage of those fates colliding to use her get-out-of-jail-free card.

While the witches were working on putting Biddy back

where she belonged, and perfectly happy to believe that it was Biddy who'd done the killing and my fault she'd been freed, I liked the idea that the vampires would help me search out more human motives and alibis.

"What else do you know about Brenda O'Donnell?" Lady Cork asked.

I tried to think. "I was at her father's wake." I paused, trying to pull the event back into my mind. Who had I seen? What had I witnessed?

The trouble was, I'd had that awful experience of my own, the scary witch face in the mirror and the go-away message. I did not wish to share that with the vampires because it was pretty compelling evidence that Biddy O'Donnell might be Brenda's killer. I didn't want to cloud their judgment or their belief that a human had committed the murder. Unfortunately, it meant I hadn't been as observant as I might have been at the wake.

I told them about the argument I'd witnessed between Brenda and Jack. The old schoolteacher that had so impressed me marching out there and telling him to go away when he had every intention of coming inside.

"There was something odd, though," I said. It wasn't someone who had been there, but someone who hadn't that puzzled me. "Dylan McAuliffe, the man Brenda was engaged to, didn't come to her father's wake." I thought about it. Even though we hadn't been married anymore, I'd gone to my ex-husband's mother's funeral. I'd gone to support Greg, as had his wife, Emily, and their two daughters. It was what you did. You supported the people you cared about when they lost loved ones. So why hadn't the man she was planning to spend the rest of her life with bothered to turn up for her father's wake and funeral?

"Good. A second suspect."

"Who inherits?" asked Lady Cork.

"I don't know. I suppose, when her father died, she, being the only child, must have inherited everything he had. That house is a bit rundown, but it's beautiful. That's got to be worth something. That would have come to Brenda, and then I suppose she would have had some assets, being a successful solicitor in Dublin."

"Follow the money," Bartholomew said, still eager to be involved. "Plenty of people have killed over inheritances. In my third novel, Day of Revenge, the Colombian drug kingpin Alphonse—"

"Excellent point, Bartholomew," Deirdre said, before Oscar could attack poor Bartholomew with his acid tongue. "We can find out the next of kin. Has her will turned up?"

Not that I'd heard. No one else had either.

I agreed that I would find out what I could and so would the vampires. I felt better just having this book club that was clearly on my side.

"Thank you," I said.

"You're very welcome. Now, get your book and let's get back to our book discussion. This is a book club, remember, not therapy," Deirdre reminded me.

I had to smile. "You're right." I turned to Lady Cork. "I think you were talking about revenge?"

CHAPTER 11

*R*evenge had been the subject at the vampire book club, and I was still thinking about it and whether the witch Biddy O'Donnell was exacting it on the living. I was alone in the Blarney Tome with no other company than my dark thoughts when Jack Buckley walked in. Never had I been sorrier to have no other customers. The last time I'd seen Jack, he'd been trying to get into Billy O'Donnell's wake and upsetting both Brenda O'Donnell and the old teacher.

He might have an alibi for Brenda's murder, but in my eyes, he was still the most likely culprit. I didn't know what he wanted with me, but I didn't relish being alone with him.

All I knew about him was that he was a drug addict, a convicted killer, and he'd spent eight years in jail and then blamed the woman whose life he'd all but ruined for his own problems. Nothing about that made me wish to know him better. So I put on my coldest professional voice. "May I help you?"

There is a way of saying "May I help you?" that's the

equivalent to "Come in, take your time, browse through all my books," and there's a way of saying "May I help you?" that's pretty much "Get the hell out of my store." Naturally, I gave him the latter version.

He walked in a few steps and then stood there looking around as though he'd never been inside a bookstore before. From what I knew of him, that might well be true.

I never took my eyes off him. I had my phone nearby, and I knew that if I yelled or screamed, someone would likely hear me. I could also stop him with magic. Though I preferred not to do that. I was trying to live like a regular person in Ballydehag and not be known as that crazy woman who could make strange things happen.

He put his hands in his pockets and took them out. Shuffled from one foot to the other. And then, when I got out of my own head, I realized he looked intensely uncomfortable. Nervous, even. I didn't thaw exactly, but I opened myself to the possibility that he wasn't here to do me harm. I said, in a marginally softer tone, "Can I help you with something?"

"I don't know." He sounded as conflicted at being here as I felt having him here. "I heard that you were there. With Brenda. At the end."

What on earth could he possibly want? I had no reason to lie, so I said, "I was. Not right at the end, but I found her after she'd been attacked and left for dead."

He shut his eyes briefly as though in pain. However, he was still number one on my list, and I suspected the Guards' list of probable suspects. Was he sorry? Maybe he'd been high at the time and was trying to figure out what he'd done?

"I'm so sorry." I had no idea who he was apologizing to.

"Sorry for what?"

"Sorry that she ended like that. Sorry I never got a chance to explain."

"Explain what?"

He rocked back and forth on his heels. His hands were still in his pockets, and he started jingling his change.

While I was still trying to formulate a response that would be both neutral and encourage him to leave the Blarney Tome immediately, he turned around and walked back toward the door. I'd barely got halfway through my sigh of relief when I watched him take the open sign and flip it around. Before I could even squawk or ask what he thought he was doing, he'd shut the door and locked it.

He turned back toward me and came three steps closer.

I pushed down the panic. He might be big and tough, but I had powers he knew nothing about. Instead of tossing him across the room or putting up a barrier he couldn't cross, I looked at him. Really looked at him and opened myself up. And what I felt wasn't threat or anger, it was pain. It was sadness.

"I can't talk properly if people are coming and going," he said by way of explanation.

"I'll give you five minutes, because this is a business, and it's supposed to be open." I didn't even own it. I was running the shop for someone else.

He nodded as though he thought that was fair. And then there was silence. I could feel him trying to find the right words. Finally, he said, "Has anyone told you about me?"

I would not play dumb. "You mean how you got Brenda O'Donnell, who was a straight-A student destined for college, into drugs? You mean how you killed another drug dealer and went to prison?"

He nodded, and I could see his eyes were full of pain. "I did do all those things. But I've changed."

And how often had every woman heard those words?

I let him see I wasn't buying it.

"No. I really have. Yes, I was furious that Brenda didn't save me like she said she would. She was meant to go to law school and then use her new profession to get me out of jail."

"And I'm guessing she was, what, seventeen or eighteen years old when she had that marvelous idea?"

He nodded briefly. "About that. But I wasn't much older. And believe me, prison isn't where anybody wants to spend the better part of a decade. It was all I lived for, thinking she'd get me out."

If he thought I would be sympathetic, he was bleating to the wrong audience. I don't know how long he would have gone on laying on this sob story, but I stopped him by saying, "Brenda O'Donnell is dead. Murdered. Tell me why I should stop believing that you killed her?"

He took a step backward. Good. Probably he was ready to run before he ended up back in that prison he hated so much.

"Because I didn't kill her. That's what I'm trying to tell you."

"I saw you arguing with her the day of her father's wake."

"I wasn't arguing with her. Well, I was, but not about her not getting me out of jail." He rocked back on his heels again. He must think the change in his pocket would have babies if he kept jingling it. "I was trying to make amends."

Now I looked at him more keenly. I'd heard those words before. Who hadn't? Everybody who's had a loved one or former friend in AA or one of the many offshoots of that recovery program knew those words well. "I'm listening."

He shook his head. "I'm clean now. In a twelve-step program. It didn't even happen in the nick, like you'd think it would. Oh, they tried. We were always getting do-gooders to come in and try to save us. No, it was after I got out. After I finished being furious at Brenda for not saving me. I got a job fixing cars, and I'm good at it, but the owner warned me that if he caught me doing drugs, I'd be out on me arse. I don't know. Maybe the wasted years didn't seem so wasted once I was out again. What was the point being angry all the time and looking backward? I saw a sign on the church door. That's what started me. And I thought, what did I have to lose? So I went to one meeting. And there were blokes like me in there. Talking about what rubbish they'd made of their lives. But there was hope, too. I know how it sounds, but it's true. And one of the steps we have to make is going back to the people you've hurt. Telling them you're sorry. Trying to make amends."

"And that's what you were doing in her father's garden? The day of his wake?"

This guy had some real timing issues.

"I didn't intend to do it then. I wanted to pay my respects. But when she stopped me going in, I tried to tell her about the amends."

I remembered seeing Brenda's face. And then that teacher barreling past me. I didn't think it had gone well. "What did Brenda say?"

"She wouldn't even listen. I was trying to tell her, and she was just telling me to go away. Maybe I could have got through to her, but that old biddy of a teacher pushed her way in and started snarling at me too. So I left."

I was certain there was more to this story. "And did you try to talk to Brenda again?"

He closed his eyes, and his chin dropped toward his sternum. He didn't speak, just nodded. Two sharp jerks of his chin up and down.

"When? When did you try to talk to her?"

His gaze came up and met mine briefly and then dropped again as though there was something much more interesting on the floor. "That day."

I had no time for games. "Which day?"

"The day she died."

"What time were you there?" Okay, I wasn't a cop, but he was here and talking, and I might as well find out what I could. The Gardaí weren't the only ones trying to figure out what had happened to Brenda O'Donnell.

"It was about four o'clock."

And I had found her barely alive a little after seven.

I wouldn't rush to condemn him. He was here, talking to me, trying to get me on his side, but I wouldn't make a snap judgment. That wouldn't be fair. "Did you see her?"

He shook his head. "It's what I regret the most. If she was going to die that night, at least I wish she would have forgiven me."

"You'd better tell me what happened."

He looked up, half-eager. "So you believe me?"

"Not even the slightest bit. You have to convince me. And there's about two minutes left of your five, and I've watched a gentleman walk back and forth in front of the door two or three times already."

"I pulled up in front of the house. I was nervous, right?"

I nodded. I could only imagine how nervous he must have been if he was telling me the truth. Trying to get forgiveness from someone whose life you nearly destroyed can't be easy for anyone. Especially somebody who was so cocky and full of pride as I sensed this one was.

"I'd just about worked up my nerve. I saw her come out of the house. She had boxes, and she was putting them in the back of a moving van. I opened the door of my truck. I had one foot already on the road when a snazzy sports car pulled up."

"A snazzy sports car? In Ballydehag?" The closest I'd seen to a sports car was Sean Higgins's Mercedes Coupe that had to be twenty years old. Maybe it had been mildly sporty at the turn of the millennium, but it had seen better days.

He shook his head at me. "Not a local car. City like."

"Go on."

As though he felt his time with me running out like sand through an hourglass, he spoke more quickly. "A bloke got out. All shiny and spiffy."

"Really? What did he look like?"

He shrugged as though he'd already described the man to perfection. "City like. Short hair styled all fancy. A suit like a banker's. Shiny loafers. His watch was probably worth more than everything I own."

At the word watch, I glanced up. I had a sneaking suspicion I knew who he was talking about.

"And what did he do? This slick stranger in a sporty car?"

"He walked up to Brenda. Tried to kiss her, but she was carrying a heavy box to put into the back of her van." He shook his head. "I didn't like him on sight, but when he didn't even take the box out of her hands, I decided he was a right twit."

I had to agree. I thought the man in front of me might have many failings, but I suspected he would have hefted Brenda's heavy moving boxes into the back of her van for her.

"Then what happened?"

He put his hands out, which at least stopped the jingling of change in his pockets. "They went inside."

That was interesting, if true. He had to be talking about the fiancé, Dylan McAuliffe, who'd told me he'd only arrived after Brenda was already on her way to the hospital. One of these two was lying. Which was it?

"Did you try to see her again?"

He shook his head. "I wish I had. But I thought I'd try the next morning. She wasn't going to leave that night, that was certain."

There was a sheen in his eyes that, in another man, could have been the threat of tears. "And I never saw her again." I felt his pain now, like a punch to my chest. "You always think there'll be another chance. You never think an everyday conversation, or a few heated words in a sunny garden on the day of a wake, will be the last time you ever speak to a person you once loved. I thought there was time. I thought I'd have another chance to make it right."

I didn't know whether he was telling the truth or lying or was just a consummate actor, but I knew that feeling so well. There were so many things I wished I'd said to the people I'd loved who were gone. To Greg, to my mother, even to my father, wherever he was.

"I was able to make it right with Billy, at least."

"With Brenda's father?"

He nodded. "I heard he was poorly, and I managed to see him before he died. He was up in his bedroom reading an old history book. Didn't look too pleased to see me, but I said my piece, how sorry I was, and we chatted a bit. He forgave me. Then I promised him I'd never hurt Brenda again and do everything I could to make amends to her." He rubbed at his eyes. "Did a rubbish job at that, though, didn't I?"

His feelings were sincere, but was he sorry that he'd never made his amends to Brenda? Or was he sorry now that he'd ended her life? Possibly without meaning to, but you didn't pick up a heavy candlestick and bash a woman over the back of the head by accident.

CHAPTER 12

*L*ater that night, someone banged on my door. It was strange because my cottage was just that far out of town that people didn't really come out without an invitation. If I were back in Seattle, I would suspect Jehovah's Witnesses or somebody wondering if my roof needed doing or my house needed painting. But that had never happened to me here. I went to the door of my cottage and opened it. It was always possible that Kathleen had come by. Or, even worse, that Pendress Kennedy had decided to pay me a visit. But when I opened the door, I saw a most surprising sight.

There was an old woman standing on the doorstep. She was stoop-shouldered and dressed in rags. I know that sounds dramatic, but she actually was dressed in rags. Her long dress was a drab color that was neither black nor gray, but some depressing color that was neither one nor the other. The hem was dirty and ragged. Her shoes looked to be wooden. Like clogs. She wore a shawl over her thin, gray hair, and her face was old and careworn. A powerful scent of body odor and earth emanated from her. I took a step back. "Can I help you?"

She glanced up at me with old, rheumy eyes. "Alms for the poor?" she said in a weak, querulous voice. She held out her two hands, and they were curved like claws.

I stood there for a minute, staring. Finally, I let my disbelief out in a snort. "Are you kidding me? Alms for the poor? What do you take me for?"

Her old eyes connected with mine, and I saw the look of deep cunning in them. Then she hastily dropped her gaze to her hands. "I'm but a poor, old woman."

"First, no one's asked for alms for the poor in hundreds of years." I was really going to have to bone up on my Irish history. I knew there'd been nothing but trouble here, from potato famines to an interminable modern conflict that they now termed "the troubles." Poverty had dogged Ireland the way mosquitoes dogged summer camp.

I might be American and modern, but alms for the poor? She was having me on. "What do you really want?"

That crafty look came and went again. "I'm but a poor old woman, mistress. Have pity."

"And I'm not your mistress. I'm pretty sure the meaning of that word has changed since you last used it."

I knew this woman was probably a terrible force for evil, but she looked so ridiculous on my doorstep, I couldn't really take it seriously. "You're Biddy O'Donnell, aren't you?"

She made a sound as though she was sucking her teeth. "I believe I've come to the wrong house. Beg your pardon."

And she backed away. I watched her all the way to the end of my garden. When she passed the wishing well, she glared at it as though she might spit in it, but knowing I was watching, she kept walking. She walked with a limp. It was the kind of limp I'd seen amateur actors use when playing someone crippled.

Once she was all the way down my garden, she disappeared. I shut the door and locked it.

Cerridwen came wandering down from upstairs as though wondering who was at the door. "You don't even want to know," I told her. I'd suspected Biddy O'Donnell was on the loose, but having it confirmed wasn't great news. I would have to tell Kathleen and Pendress about my evening visitor. Kathleen would probably be supportive, but Pendress would somehow make the rising of the old witch seem like my fault.

I didn't have the strength to face them tonight. Tomorrow would be soon enough.

I was thinking about a bath in the big tub upstairs, with a glass of wine and some soothing herbs, when there was another knock on my door. I had a strong suspicion it was that strange, old woman back again. What on earth did she want this time? I could have ignored the door and probably should have, but if nothing else, she had excited my curiosity.

Still, I flipped on all the lights on my way to the front door. Then I opened it. I was halfway through my, "May I help you?" when my tongue caught in my throat. I got out something that sounded like, "May I hell..." and then I sounded like someone choking on their tongue.

Standing in front of me was a beautiful woman. She had to be at least six feet tall. She had long, wavy, red hair, a face that ought to grace a glossy magazine cover, and a figure that ought to grace a Playboy centerfold. She wore a shimmery blue dress that I'd love to have if I was ever going to a costume party. Instead of wooden clogs, this vision wore black, patent leather, high-heeled shoes. Her ankles wobbled with the effort of holding herself up in them. At the edge of the wishing well in my front garden, I saw a shadow move. I didn't think it was Cerridwen, because she was upstairs asleep.

I said again, "May I help you?" managing to get the entire sentence out this time.

"Yes," she said in a breathy voice. "I wonder if I might use your telephone?"

I stared at her and as I did, her neck shifted slightly and her head wobbled as though it was about to fall off her shoulders.

"Are you all right?"

She grabbed her head with both hands and pushed it back on top of her neck properly. "Yes, I'm fine. I've had an accident with my motorcar. I wonder if I might use your telephone?"

Again, I didn't know what else to do than laugh. "Where is your motorcar now?" I asked her. Okay, maybe it was unkind of me to toy with her, but she was seriously messing with my head.

"Just over there." She gestured vaguely behind her.

I gave her my most skeptical look. She gazed back at me with limpid blue eyes, but there was a moment when the image shifted and the wicked, old hag stared at me. The rest remained the same: long red hair, the gorgeous dress, even those ridiculous heels. It was just the face. As though she was putting so much effort into keeping the illusion going that it was thin in places, so thin I'd been able to see right through it.

"I'm getting tired of this, Biddy O'Donnell. What do you want from me?"

She pursed up her lips as though she planned to cling to her ridiculous story. I rolled my gaze. "First, nobody has a motorcar anymore. You just say car. And yes, we use the telephone, but most people would call it the phone. And, frankly, pretty much everyone has a mobile here. That's a phone you hold in your hand. It's wonderful. You can take them anywhere. So it really takes away the need to knock on a complete stranger's door and ask for help."

For a moment more she clung to her illusion, and then with a great huff of disgust, she let me see the real her. Frankly, it wasn't pretty.

Biddy O'Donnell was a short, scrawny witch. Her hair was gray and thin, and her face looked like one of those dried apple dolls. Her black eyes were darting, as though trying to catch something in a corner. Her clothes weren't as ragged as the image she'd presented to me earlier, when she'd pretended to be a beggar, but they were old-fashioned. She wore a long—I suppose you'd call it a smock which went to the ground, and she still wore those wooden clogs. There was a cap on her head and a shawl wrapped around her shoulders. If she was a character in a period drama, she'd be a servant or a common woman out in the streets.

"I see," she said finally, sounding irritable. "You're not as stupid as you look."

"Not nearly."

"And you've identified me correctly. I am that very Biddy

O'Donnell. And you are the child of my child's child's child's child's child's child."

I found this very hard to believe. No, I wanted to find this very hard to believe, but something inside me recognized our kinship. It was probably why I'd been able to see through her from the beginning.

Probably it was a very dangerous thing to invite an ancient, evil witch into my home, but hey, she was family. I held the door open and beckoned for her to enter. She stepped past me with great dignity. She still smelled like body odor and dirt. I was about to close the door behind her when a black shape shot past me. I jumped back.

The old woman clucked her tongue. "What are you so startled for? It's only Pyewacket."

The streak of black resolved itself into a cat. And, like my many times grandmother Biddy O'Donnell, Pyewacket had seen better days. Its fur was matted and lank, one of its eyes drooped, and half of one ear was missing. As though I had not gathered this, she said, "Pyewacket's my familiar."

I led the pair of them into my living room, not knowing what else to do with them, and offered them a seat. Biddy O'Donnell sat in my nicest chair, and I thought I would have to get it steam-cleaned when she left. The cat sniffed its way around the room, very much the way Cerridwen would do, but when it saw the length of colored wool that I used when I was playing with Cerridwen, flicking it around and driving her into a frenzy, the cat arched its back and let out a hideous shriek. Its head went one way and its body the other. I'd never seen anything so peculiar in my life.

The old woman got up and went toward the cat. She took its little head and shifted it like a chiropractor making a spinal adjustment. "You must leave nothing lying around that reminds her of rope. She had a terrible experience."

I looked at her and looked at her cat. They both had that weird shifting head thing. I felt a bit sick. "You don't mean?"

I couldn't even finish the sentence, but she finished it for me. "Oh yes. We were both convicted of witchcraft. And both of us were hanged."

I felt an icy shiver of creepiness go over my entire body. "They executed your cat?"

She nodded grimly. "Hanging breaks your neck. Neither of us have ever been right since."

"But you're a powerful witch. Can't you fix it?"

She glared at me. "You try having your neck broken and then being shoved upside-down in a grave for hundreds of years. Let's see how you turn out."

She returned to her seat and looked me over. "So you're my great-great-great-great-great-great-great-granddaughter," she said, not sounding very impressed.

"I'm not that great."

"That's clear."

I remembered that she was a dark witch and there were rumors that she'd done terrible things. Once more, I said, "What do you want?"

"I want my house back, for a start."

Oh, no, not my pretty cottage that I'd grown to love. "You lived here?" She could have it if it was hers because I would not fight her for it, not with the creepy stunts she'd been pulling.

"No. I don't want this place."

That was good. I wondered if maybe I could do us both a favor and get her to scram to somewhere far away. "Most of the people around here who've heard the legends want you back underground."

Her faced pinched, and a sour look crossed it. "I blame Shakespeare," she said.

"What?" I don't know what I'd expected she might say, but that was not it.

"All that Macbeth nonsense." And then she hunched her already humped back and put her already claw-like hands into even worse claws and scrunched her scrunchy face even more and rasped in her already raspy voice, "Double, double toil and trouble," and then she leaned back. "That's what gave our kind a terrible name. The man would do anything to sell seats to his terrible plays. Even make lovely, kind healers like ourselves look like evil villains."

It was a solid argument, and most thinking, modern people accepted that the witch trials had mostly been a sham. Mostly. I stared at her. "I don't think Shakespeare made up the notion of the dark witch. I've heard some pretty awful tales about you."

Those black gaze shifted to the ground and then back up to meet mine. She couldn't help herself. A smug smile tilted the corners of her wrinkled mouth. "What tales have you heard?"

"Bad things. Give me one good reason why I shouldn't work with the rest of the coven to put you back in the ground?"

Her gaze was steely. "I'll give you two reasons. One, you are part of a terrible prophecy. And if we're to stop Bally-dehag from being destroyed, you'll need my help."

Okay, that was bad enough. There were two things? I wasn't even sure I wanted to hear the second. I said nothing, just stared at her. It was possible that my jaw had become unhinged and was hanging down on my chest.

She didn't wait for me to ask. She said, with relish, "And the second reason is, without my help, you'll be the next one to die."

CHAPTER 13

"*A*re you planning to kill me? Like you killed poor Brenda O'Donnell? Because I should tell you, I'm not without power mIyself."

Her tone was peevish. "Why would I kill my own kin?" Then she paused. "I don't mean husbands." As though they were expendable, which, to her, it seemed they had been. "You're my flesh and blood, girl."

And I'd have taken flesh and blood from a lot of other places before I'd ever want hers.

"I will not kill you. And I didn't kill that other gal, either."

I was very relieved to hear this. I really hoped it turned out to be true.

"I've nowhere to stay tonight," she said. "Have you a guest room?"

I didn't think Biddy O'Donnell had ever slept in a guest room in her life. And she wouldn't be bedding down in mine.

I shook my head. "It's too dangerous. The coven knows you're free, and they want to put you back." I didn't say, "where you belong," but the words echoed anyway, unsaid. It wasn't really an excuse. If Pendress Kennedy and Kathleen McGinnis got so much as a whiff of my not-so-illustrious ancestor, they'd be throwing every spell they had to get rid of her. I wasn't sure they were wrong. She sniffed. "Fine. I'll go back to the house on the hill."

I was immediately suspicious. "What house on the hill?"

She looked at me like I was being particularly stupid. "Where the man died. And his daughter."

And speaking of the house on the hill... "It was you, wasn't it? The hideous face in the mirror. And you who wrote that horrible message on the mirror telling me to go home."

"Yes. It was me."

"But why? If you've got some prophecy that says you and I need to work together to prevent obliteration, why would you try to send me home?"

"I was annoyed. I wanted to get your attention. And I suppose I wanted to see what you'd do. If you turned tail and ran home again, then you wouldn't be able to stand against dark forces, now would you?"

I supposed that made sense. "So you've been sleeping in Brenda O'Donnell's house?"

She made a sound that was half growl, half shriek. "It was mine long before it was hers." Her fury passed as suddenly as it had risen. "Besides, haven't the beds come a long way since I was mortal? So comfortable. She's got something called a Tempur-Pedic. I don't know what it is, but I've had the best night's sleep I've had in years. Centuries."

I had a feeling that anything would be an improvement on being stood on your broken head in a bunch of dirt under a massive stone, but I kept that feeling to myself.

I was very confused. I looked at her sitting, small and

wizened and looking at me out of those crafty, old eyes. What did she really want? Finally, I came right out and asked her. "If you have that nice Tempur-Pedic bed to sleep in in the O'Donnell residence, why would you want to stay here in my little, humble cottage?" My cottage really wasn't that humble, but I was pushing the idea.

She cackled. The thing about witches is we've come a long way in hundreds of years. We don't wear pointy hats, most of us don't have warts on our noses, and we don't cackle. Biddy O'Donnell had a lot to learn about the modern witch. When she'd finished cackling, she said, "I need you to buy my house back for me."

Fingers of icy dread walked their way down my spine. My horror must have shown on my face, for she cackled again. I shook my head. "You're not thinking of staying in Ballydehag, are you?"

"Where else would I go? This is my home. You will buy the house on the hill so I'll be safe. We're kin, after all."

I really needed to get this straight. "Are you suggesting that we live together?" I could not think of any worse fate. She would literally be the roommate from hell.

She didn't look thrilled to live with me either. "It's the only way I can have what's rightfully mine."

"I don't want to be rude about this, but I don't think you have the right to property. You've been dead for hundreds of years." I thought about it. "Besides, that house can't be more than two hundred years old. It couldn't have been yours."

She looked annoyed. Her little, wizened face got even more pinched, and I could hear the snapping of her few remaining teeth banging together. "They burned down my house."

I felt my eyes open wide. "Who burned down your house?"

"They hated me. And they'll hate you, too. You try to live peacefully and be a good witch, but they always have their eyes on you. And at the slightest deviation, they'll come after you like a pack of hungry wolves."

"Who's they?"

She snorted. "The regular folk. But don't be fooled. Some of your witches will turn on you too."

A vision of Pendress Kennedy flashed across my mind. She seemed like she might turn on me if I didn't toe the line.

"Is it true what they say about you?"

She sat up very straight. Being that she was quite short, her head still didn't reach the top of the chair back. "Of course, it's not true." Then she shifted a little, and those black eyes gleamed. "What do they say?"

On top of what Kathleen had told me, I'd done some research on my computer. My training as a law librarian was coming in surprisingly useful, and I'd found some very interesting old documents. "You were accused of murdering your husbands. And, also, taking away a woman's bloom of youth prematurely. And finally, for consorting with the devil."

She banged her foot on the flagstone floor, and since she was wearing those wooden clogs, it made quite a racket. "Scurrilous lies." She shook her head at me so the thin, gray wisps of her hair floated about. "I had three husbands. Is it my fault they were weaklings? And because I became a wealthy woman, the townspeople decided I was consorting with the devil. They couldn't accept that a woman could run an excellent business on her own. If she didn't have a husband behind her, it must be the devil."

I had some sympathy for her. Women's rights had come a long way even in the last fifty years. I couldn't imagine what it had been like in her time. I was willing to give her the benefit of the doubt on those. "But what about the accusation that you stole the bloom of youth away from another woman?"

Again with that terrible cackle. "That one's true. She was so very proud of her long, flowing, red hair. I might have let her be if she hadn't insulted me."

"What did you do?"

"I put a curse on her. Her hair fell out. Every last hair on her head. It was most satisfying."

Note to self. Do not get on the wrong side of Biddy O'Donnell.

I said, "Biddy, if the other witches find out you're here, they will put you back in the ground again." There had been no doubt that was Pendress Kennedy's intention. Mine too, truth be told. Though, now that I was having a conversation with this old witch, I hesitated to do anything so brutal. But what else were we going to do with her? "You can't stay here. Why don't you go to a different part of Ireland?"

"I've just told you. This is my home. And I want my house back. Well, not my house, because they burned that down, but I quite like the one they put in its place. You buy that and move into it, and you'll barely notice I'm there. Perhaps stay away from the upper floor."

"I can't afford the O'Donnell house."

She had no patience for my excuses. "Do what I did. Do what women have always done. Marry a man of good fortune. Find a stupid one with lots of money. You can lead him around by his nose with a little magic."

She was such a romantic! "I am not getting married so you can have your house back."

She made a hissing noise and then, to my shock, flames came out of her ears and her nostrils and licked up over her hair. Muttering with annoyance, she slapped the flames back down again. "Now look what you made me do!" she said in a querulous voice. They hadn't been metaphorical flames either. They'd been real. She'd singed her own hair.

She was really not selling herself as a roommate.

"We don't even know who that house is going to yet. It depends what Brenda O'Donnell's will says. For all we know, whoever inherits it will want to keep it."

She cackled again. "Not when I'm finished with them." I thought about how she had terrified me with her face leering at me from the mirror and then writing that go-away message. And she had wanted me to stay. I couldn't imagine what she was capable of if she was trying to get rid of somebody, and I really didn't want to find out.

"It's not ideal, but you must buy the house. At any rate," the old woman said, "you'll be quieter than that mob that's been around there."

I looked at her in confusion. "What mob? Do you mean at the O'Donnell house?"

"Aye. There have been all sorts of comings and goings. A body can barely get a wink of sleep."

I felt my heart speed up. I didn't want her to know how much I cared about her information, so I kept my voice casual, skeptical even, as though I suspected she was making up stories. "Who's been there?"

"That skinny redhead, for a start. Creeping around the place." That had to be Brenda O'Donnell, who had a lot more legal right to be in the O'Donnell residence than this old witch did. "And that dandy of a fellow."

Now she really had my attention. "What dandy of a fellow?"

"Polished as fine as a five-pence piece, he was. And with a timepiece around his wrist that glittered. Solid gold it was. You mark my words."

I knew one person who fit that description. Funny how everyone noticed that fancy watch. "When did you see him?"

At this she grew vague. "How would I know? I'm a frail, old woman with failing eyesight."

Okay, Biddy O'Donnell probably didn't have the latest cell phone or digital wristwatch. "Did you see him before or after the red-haired woman died?"

Again she seemed very vague. "And then there was a box with tiny people coming and going. Making such a racket. Worse than leprechauns, they were."

Suddenly I got where she'd come up with that sexy, femme fatale persona she'd put on for my benefit. "That's called a television. And that woman you imitated was from an old movie. That's like a play," I explained to her. I didn't have the time or energy to get into the whole moving pictures thing. She'd figure it out soon enough. Or, better still, she'd be back where there was no such thing.

I wanted to press her more about what she'd seen and heard inside the O'Donnell house. It hadn't occurred to me that she might be a terrible old witch but was also a witness to what had gone on in that house. I was about to question her further when there was a terrible shriek from upstairs. We both looked around. Sure enough, Pyewacket was missing.

I ran up the stairs to find two furious, black familiars staring each other down. Both had their backs arched and were hissing. Pyewacket's head had fallen to one side again, but it made her no less fierce. With that half an ear and the wonky eye, she looked like a fighter who never gives up. I was about to pick up Cerridwen when Pyewacket made an unearthly howl and, leaping into the air, threw herself, claws out, at my cat.

I put up my hand and yelled, "Stop!" I wasn't sure how well my magic worked on someone else's familiar, but I was gratified when the cat froze in midair. The old witch huffed and puffed up the stairs behind me and came in just in time to see her familiar hanging in space, its jaws open in a howl of rage.

She muttered, "No need to get angry." Then she stomped over and plucked her familiar out of the air. I dropped the magic, and Pyewacket meowed pathetically, as though complaining that she was the victim here. Cerridwen looked at me, and one of her eyes closed all the way and opened again. I could have sworn that cat was winking at me.

From the way Biddy O'Donnell was fussing over her familiar, I had a bit of a brainwave. I said, "Obviously, we can't live together if our familiars can't get along. They're sworn enemies. So it would never work."

She squinted at me out of her old eyes and said, "We'll see about that."

What was that supposed to mean? It sounded vaguely like a threat. Cats were territorial, familiars more so. Was she suggesting that one of us would get rid of our familiars? I decided to keep a careful eye on Cerridwen.

It was getting late, and I told the witch I had to go to bed. I had work in the morning.

"Very well. I bid you farewell." And then, black cat tucked under her arm, she left by the front door. I stood at the window and watched to make sure she left. I wasn't even the tiniest bit surprised when she grabbed a ragged, old wicker broom and, cat settled in front of her, took off into the night sky.

CHAPTER 14

The next day I was working on accounts. I couldn't get my numbers to add up right. I couldn't concentrate. I couldn't stop thinking about my long-lost ancestor, who I really wished had stayed lost, and poor Brenda O'Donnell. Biddy O'Donnell claimed she hadn't killed Brenda. Did I believe her? And was the old woman telling the truth? Had the fiancé come back? What was he doing in Brenda's house when she was dead? Did he even have a legal right to be there?

That last day, Brenda had brought me her books. I had a hunch she had also taken Karen Tate the smaller items that she'd planned to sell through Granny's Drawers. I wondered if they'd spoken. Had Karen seen anything? I'd clear my head and pay my fellow shopkeeper a visit.

I had discovered that it was common among local shopkeepers to just put up a sign saying we'd be back soon if we had other places to be. Few of us could afford a second employee. So I put my "back in fifteen minutes" sign up after looking both ways to make sure there was nobody headed straight for my shop. There wasn't.

It was a warm, sunny day, and it felt good to be outside. The bakery was still closed, and I felt a pang of sadness. The butcher was doing an excellent business, but I'd taken to avoiding it the way Sean and Rosie Higgins avoided my bookshop. Feelings were still too raw. However, Tara was outside serving coffee to a couple sitting at a table on the patio of the Cork Coffee Company. She gave me a cheerful wave as I walked by. I had to remember, not everybody hated me. I waved back and continued on. When I got to Granny's Drawers, Kathleen McGinnis was coming out. We met on the sidewalk outside.

"Quinn," she said. "I've been meaning to come by and see you. How are you getting on?" She dropped her voice and added, "No more trouble with the yew then?"

I shook my head. "Everything seems quiet." I was tempted for only a moment to tell her about my visit from Biddy O'Donnell, but some instinct stopped me. I didn't know why I felt wary of my sister witch, I only knew that I did. She looked at my face searchingly. No doubt she could tell there was something I wasn't saying. But she didn't push.

"I popped in to have a good rummage through the O'Donnell family leftovers. But, would you believe it, Karen hasn't unpacked a single box yet. Says she's been too busy." She shook her head. "She'll never make much money in that shop if she doesn't put out her stock, now will she?"

"No. She won't."

"No doubt that's what you were after too."

I gave a slight laugh. "Who doesn't like a good rummage?"

At least I now had an excuse for why I was here. "Well, Karen's seen me now, so I'd better go in."

"All right. I'd best get back to my shop too. Heaven only knows what Danny will have done while I'm gone."

At least she had someone she could leave in charge, even if it was a doddery, old man. I would have to look into part-time help at the bookstore. Sure, it would lessen my earnings, but it would free up some time for other pursuits, such as getting rid of evil, ancient witches.

I walked into Granny's Drawers and was pleased to find I was the only customer in the shop. Karen Tate immediately came over. "Quinn. Good to see you."

"You, too." I didn't want to bring up the Brenda murder, hoping she would. I said, "It was so nice getting out for dinner with you the other night. We must do it again."

She nodded, then looked sad. "What a shame Brenda didn't come with us that night. Now we'll never have the chance."

I nodded, suitably somber. But I was pleased that she had brought up the subject. "I saw her that last day. She brought books over from her father's collection." I made a face. "Mostly a lot of junk, to be honest."

I waited. This was her chance to tell me whatever had transpired between them, but she merely nodded. "I'm not surprised. Billy had some very peculiar hobbies. He loved Roman history and Byzantine architecture, and I think he was a train-spotter."

She was correct. I nodded. "Also old thrillers."

She didn't mention having seen Brenda that last day, but I knew she must have because I'd seen those boxes labeled all ready for her.

"What about you?" I asked. If she wouldn't volunteer the information, I'd go after it. "Did she have anything good for you?"

She looked for a moment as though she didn't know what I was talking about. Then seemed to recollect. "Oh. That old junk of her dad's. I've no idea. I've got a few boxes upstairs, but frankly, I think most of it's worthless."

That surprised me. "That bad?" I hadn't really looked that carefully, but it had seemed to me from the stuff I'd seen crammed in the china cabinets alone that some of it had value.

I'd come here thinking we'd compare notes, see if either of us could think of a motive for Brenda's murder, but I sensed Karen had put up a wall. She'd no intention of sharing information. In fact, she kept looking past me out into the road as though she could will customers to come in and free her from this tête-à-tête.

She nearly breathed a sigh of relief when the door opened and someone came in. "Hello," she said, giving me a nod and moving out of my way. "How can I help?"

Edna and Clara, the pair of old women who lived for gossip and liked to dig for bargains, were hardly A-list customers. "We're only here to browse." And they'd both headed straight for the one-euro box Karen kept.

I couldn't talk murder in front of them, so I said, "Well, I'd better get back to my shop."

Edna pulled a frayed crocheted doily out of the box. "Oh, look at this, Clara. My aunt used to crochet. Lovely work, she did. I'm sure I've got some of her linens in the closet upstairs. I must turn it out one of these days. No doubt I've got treasures galore that you could sell for me, Karen."

I WAS all ready for the vampire book club meeting, though I was more interested in what they might have discovered about the murder than what they thought about Wilkie Collins's The Moonstone, when there was a great commotion from downstairs. Usually they were quiet when they came in. It sounded like someone was having an argument.

A man with a loud, blustery voice that I didn't recognize was shouting. Before I could investigate, a trio of vampires burst in. Well, one of them burst in and two struggled to restrain him. The central figure was a curious one. He looked like Charles II. His hair was in flowing waves around a round, ruddy face. His eyes were fierce and bloodshot. He wore a full, white shirt and breeches. He was straining toward me even as Lochlan Balfour and a young, very strong-looking vampire held him back.

He looked at me and his nose twitched as though he smelled something delicious. Instinctively, I took a step back.

"And aren't you a delectable, tasty colleen," he said, looking at me and licking his lips.

I felt some alarm, even though I knew how powerful Lochlan was. Instinctively, I gazed at him.

"My apologies," he said. "This is Thomas Blood. We don't normally let him come out with us. And this is Desmond Cronin, who usually keeps him company during the book club meetings. But Thomas has some information you might find useful."

Thomas Blood made a sound like a man about to rush into battle. "Not let me out much? They keep me a prisoner.

Chained up in the dungeon, I am." He pointed a finger at the young vampire. "With him as my jailer."

Lochlan shook his head. "Don't be ridiculous, Thomas. You have your own private quarters and outings every night."

"Never allowed out on my own. Might as well be chained in a dungeon."

"We cannot have you hunting. We live peacefully. You'd put us all in danger."

The man made another sound of outrage. "I like my food fresh. I do not want that cup of sustenance." He eyed me up again. "I like to hunt my food."

"You will not hunt Quinn," Lochlan said.

"That gets my vote too," I said.

Oscar came in with Deidre, and they both looked quite surprised to see Thomas Blood there. Oscar said, "What have you brought this uncouth old boor here for? Can he even read?"

Thomas Blood roared again. "I'd have had you at the end of me spit if I'd met you when you were still alive."

Oscar looked at Lochlan. "Can't you put him back in his cage? The smell of him alone is turning my stomach."

"I will if he doesn't behave," Lochlan said.

That had the effect of making Thomas Blood calm down a bit. "All right. I'll behave."

He sat, Lochlan on one side of him and Desmond on the other side. I was pretty sure I was safe, but I would keep an eye on him, anyway. Just knowing there was a vampire who preferred the old-fashioned ways around made me determined to get a nice, sharpened stick to keep in my desk drawer. Just in case. Still, I had protection spells and enough power that I could probably keep him at bay if I had to.

"Tell Quinn about Biddy O'Donnell," Lochlan Balfour said.

For the first time since he'd arrived, I warmed to Thomas Blood. "You knew my great, great, great, great, great, great grandmother?"

He looked at me like he was having trouble counting all the greats. "I knew Biddy O'Donnell, aye. Dreadful old crone."

Yep, sounded like we were talking about the same person. "What do you know about her?"

"She ran an inn. It was the only one for miles. She was a notorious skinflint, overcharged for flea-bitten quarters, where the sheets were always damp, if they'd been changed at all. She used to tell fortunes in the corner of the alehouse. Killed all three of her husbands, you know? I had an eye to her myself, but after the third went to meet his maker, I decided to keep my sword in its scabbard."

Thomas Blood seemed like an awful man, but he had known Biddy O'Donnell. He was the only witness we had, and I was grateful to Lochlan for bringing him to the bookshop, even as I hoped he wouldn't make a habit of it.

"Now that you've been around a lot longer, Mr. Blood—"

"You may call me Tom," he said with a leer.

"Tom." I had to gather my thoughts again. It was difficult to hold my focus when I could feel his gaze on my throat. "Do you really believe that she murdered her husbands?"

He seemed to give the matter serious thought. He crossed his arms across his barrel chest and sank his chin down so at least now he was contemplating the floor and not my jugular vein. "I could not tell you about the first husband. He was taken by a fever, which could be true. But the second husband, struth, he was an ugly, old blighter. It was his alehouse, mark you, and after she married him, she worked as a serving wench. She was nay so hideous in those days. Not comely, but passable. He went off in an apoplexy. Could she not have done that by magic?"

He looked at me, and I had to admit I thought she probably could have. I thought back in those days they used the term apoplexy for everything from a stroke to an epileptic fit. There were plenty of poisons that could cause a death that way.

"Possibly," I said.

"As I said, I had my eye on her at that point. They'd had no children, and she was now a wealthy widow with a good bit of property. And I was lying low myself. I'd had a venture that didn't pay off."

Lochlan chuckled. "A venture? Is that what you call it?"

Thomas Blood broke out into a broad chuckle of his own. "I was always a bold man. I had no time for half measures." He looked at me, and he was like a different man, suddenly jovial and bluff. "I nearly got away with the Crown Jewels."

It was so unexpected, even I laughed. "You stole the Crown Jewels?"

"In my very hands I had them. I had the crown about me, though I'd had to flatten it with a mallet to avoid detection. I was dressed as a parson, you see. Slipped the thing into my robes as quietly as a confession. My son had the orb, and a colleague attempted to take the scepter." He shook his head, looking suddenly heartbroken. "But the luck wasn't with us."

I thought it was astonishing they'd got that far. "I saw the Crown Jewels once, in the Tower of London." I'd had to line up for ages and then to stand on a conveyer belt and float past some of the world's most fabulous jewels. I couldn't even stop to stare as long as I wanted to.

"You're right, Mistress. That's where they stored the crown jewels even then. Though there weren't so many in those days. Still, a tidy haul."

"Mr. Blood, Tom, how were you not hanged?"

"Well, they put me in the Tower good and tight." He glared at Lochlan. "Like I'm imprisoned now. But I refused to speak to anyone but the king. That was Charles the second, you understand. He had a sense of humor, the king, I'll give him that. He sent for me, and I told him my story, and when I was finished he not only pardoned me but gave me a pension of five hundred a year."

Was he having me on? Telling tall tales for the gullible colonial? I glanced at Lochlan, but he was nodding. It must be true. Math had never been my strongest subject, but I thought a pension of five hundred a year in the reign of Charles II must have been a tidy sum.

"So you came back with your pension to hide away here in Ireland." It probably wasn't a terrible idea. He must have worried that Charles might change his mind.

"And that's when I met her last husband. Gerry O'Donnell, he was. He managed to get her with child, and then he too met with an unfortunate end."

"What happened to him?" I almost didn't want to know. If Biddy O'Donnell was my many times back grandmother, then this poor sap must be my many times back grandfather.

Thomas Blood might not have been the most successful thief, but he was a gifted storyteller. He all but rubbed his hands. "Well, now, that's a strange tale. Gerry O'Donnell had a fine business, he did. He was an ale merchant, you see. And he not only gave her the babe but a great deal of money. I suspect she had no further use for him and one day he was found drownded in a barrel of his own ale. It looked like he'd fallen in. But I always wondered. So did the rest of the town. People began to look at Biddy O'Donnell sideways. Ye used to see her, in the corner where she'd be telling her fortunes, whispering away to that black cat of hers."

A little shiver went over my spine. I knew all about that cat.

"And then they said she cursed Esther Flynt." He put his head to one side. "Esther was a comely lass with hair that flowed down her back like a fountain of gold. Powerful jealous of her, old Biddy was. And then one day the poor lass —Esther that be—lost her hair. Pitiful to see, it was, until she was as bald as a newborn babe."

"But a disease could have caused her baldness."

"It was the glee and triumph of Biddy that gave her away. I'd thought I might have a go at her myself one more time. But I had a nasty feeling. I did not want to be the fourth of her husbands to come to an untimely end. Besides, if I'd had the Crown Jewels, she probably would have taken me, but I had little more than my sword, my pension and my grand ideas to my name."

"Not to mention a wife still alive," Lochlan reminded him.

Thomas Blood waved a hand at such minor inconveniences.

I thought he'd had a lucky escape. "What happened?" I was waiting for the rest of the story.

He blinked those bloodshot eyes and looked at me. "She was hanged, wasn't she?"

"Hanged."

He nodded. "And that mangy, old cat with her. They were never separated, even on the scaffold."

My mind skittered away from that image. "What happened to the baby?" I assumed it had survived since Biddy claimed me as her kin.

"It was taken in by a local family. Name of Kennedy."

Something inside me jerked like a plucked guitar string. Kennedy was a very common name in these parts. Still, could there be a connection between me and Pendress Kennedy? It made sense that whoever took in Biddy O'Donnell's baby would likely have been a witch. I suspected in those days most of the villagers wouldn't have touched her with a ten-foot pole. I hoped the Kennedys had been kind to her, poor thing. Still, I suspected it was in her best interests not to have Biddy O'Donnell bring her up.

"What happened to the inn?" I asked.

"They burned it to the ground. Once they'd deemed that it was a place of witchcraft, the local councilors decided to burn it. Shame. It was a nice public house in its time."

"Do you remember where it was?"

He looked at me. "Aye. The land lay empty for a long time. Nobody wanted it. Young Mistress O'Donnell grew up and claimed it. She married and had children of her own. She'd taken the name Kennedy by then, but oddly she married an O'Donnell. The land's been in O'Donnell hands ever since. And one of them made a bit of money and had ideas above his station. He built that Georgian house, and it still stands today."

It was nice to have Biddy O'Donnell's story confirmed. How weird to think I had a connection with that place. I didn't like the house, though. It gave me the creeps when I was inside of it. Maybe, like the blood that ran through my veins, so did the memories of what had happened there. I was surprised Biddy O'Donnell wanted it back unless as a reminder of when she'd been alive.

I could hardly concentrate on the book. Thomas Blood enjoyed it immensely, though, as it was about stolen jewels. I kept thinking about Biddy O'Donnell and how she'd been so irked by the people invading her house. Had she been bothered enough to take a candlestick and bash Brenda O'Donnell on the back of the head?

When the meeting ended, Lochlan made sure Thomas Blood was well escorted and then remained behind to talk to me.

"I hope you didn't mind me bringing him? I thought you might find it helpful to hear about Biddy O'Donnell. Considering..."

I nodded. "Considering she nearly killed me in my own home with that spell book. Do you think she killed Brenda O'Donnell?"

"To get her house back?" He raised his hand and did a maybe, maybe not motion. "She's not a stupid witch. She must know that someone will move into that house."

"Unless she can convince the community that the house is so badly haunted that no one ever wants to move there again."

I thought she was going about it the right way, too. The house had experienced both a natural death and a murder within its walls within the past couple of weeks. I thought most people would think twice before rushing to buy it.

"She told me that there'd been a dandy in the place going through the things. She described his watch. I think the man she's referring to is Brenda O'Donnell's fiancé, Dylan McAuliffe." I paused, thinking. "At least he told me he was her fiancé. I've only his word for it."

His gaze sharpened on my face. "You think he wasn't?"

"I don't know. Why would he lie? Unless he had some other reason to be there. And if he killed her, why did he do it?"

Lochlan walked over to the window, raised the blind slightly and looked out. No doubt he was making sure Thomas Blood was being properly escorted home, which I very much appreciated. He turned. "Whatever happened to Brenda O'Donnell, it would make sense that the answer was in Dublin."

I hadn't thought of that angle, but he was right. I'd assumed that coming home had stirred old angers and enemies. Which led right to Jack the drug dealer's door. But when Jack had been to see me, I had half believed him when he insisted he hadn't killed Brenda.

"I'll do some sleuthing. Jack said he saw Dylan McAuliffe before I did, when Brenda was already on her way to the hospital. Dylan told me he'd just arrived. If that was true, he couldn't have killed her. If Jack was right, he could be our guy. I'll call the lawyer's office where they both worked. Hopefully, his assistant will know what time he left the office that day."

"Or even if he went in at all. It's about a four-hour drive from Dublin to Ballydehag if you don't stop."

"Let's see what time he left."

CHAPTER 15

*I*t felt good to have another avenue to explore. I gathered together a story that sounded plausible to me and the next morning I phoned the law offices of Fitzpatrick, Lyon, McKenzie five minutes after the offices officially opened.

I'd chosen my time deliberately. Having worked in a lawyer's office, I knew that while the assistants started right on time, the lawyers often wandered in later, after breakfast meetings or squash games. I called early because I didn't want to speak to the lawyer himself; I very much wanted to talk to his assistant.

Sure enough, they put me straight through to a pleasant-sounding woman after I had asked the switchboard operator for Dylan McAuliffe.

I asked for him again, and she said, "I'm sorry. He's not here. Can I put you through to one of our other partners who is taking his cases?"

Someone else was taking his cases? Had he decided to

take some time off while he was here? "I was really hoping to speak to him. Do you know when he'll be back in the office?"

There was a tiny pause, and then she said, "I'm sorry. He no longer works here."

"What?" The exclamation was out before I could stop myself. "This must be sudden. I'm sure he was working there last week."

"I'm afraid I can't tell you any more. Would you like me to refer your case?"

I shook my head. Then realized she couldn't see me, and said, "Could I speak to Brenda O'Donnell's assistant?"

I felt the silence between me and this stranger on the other end of the phone grow thick. Was she trying to decide whether to tell me Brenda was dead? Thinking of hanging up? Finally, she said, cool and professional, "One moment," and the line clicked. I thought she might have hung up, but a second or two passed, and another voice said, "Brenda O'Donnell's office."

I'd only had seconds to think, but I decided to tell the truth as much as I could to get some information. "Hello," I said. "My name's Quinn Callahan, and I'm calling from Ballydehag."

"Ballydehag."

"Yes. I know that Brenda O'Donnell passed away. I'm so sorry."

"Thank you."

"I have some valuable books that belong to her estate. I wonder if you know who her next of kin is?"

"I don't. No."

There was a pause. She didn't hang up, so I pushed a

little. "Should I give them to Dylan McAuliffe? He's here, and I understand he's her fiancé."

There was a sound like shuffling and then the click of a closing door. The woman said, dropping the cool, professional act, "Don't give anything to Dylan McAuliffe. He is not her fiancé." That was told in a fierce tone. I bet this woman had been a great personal assistant and was still utterly loyal to her boss. "She finished with him."

"You mean they broke up? Really? Then why is he down here telling everyone they were going to get married?"

"I can't tell you that, but I advise you not to trust him. Please don't give him anything that belonged to Brenda."

Naturally, I was pretty stunned by this news. "Who should I give the books to?" That sounded inane. I tried again. "Do you know who her beneficiary is?"

"The truth is, I'm not sure she left a will. She was young, you see." Her voice wobbled, and her grief traveled across the miles. "Likely, she thought she had lots of time."

I thanked her and ended the call. I paced up and down the ailes between the bookshelves. No doubt it would look to an outsider like I was trying to find a particular volume, but really, I was thinking.

About lies and liars. About revenge. Treasures, whether magical moonstones or rundown Georgian houses.

I now knew that Dylan could have left any time on the day of Brenda's murder or probably days before. He didn't have a job.

It seemed he also didn't have a fiancée.

And now, I wondered why Dylan McAuliffe had come to Ballydehag at all.

I went back over the facts and timelines as I knew them on the night that Brenda had died. The trouble was, I had various people's stories, but I didn't know which ones were true.

Dylan had lied about when he'd arrived, if Jack was to be believed—and he'd been poking around the O'Donnell house, if Biddy O'Donnell was to be believed. The trouble was, if there were ever two more unreliable witnesses than Jack Buckley and Biddy O'Donnell, I didn't know who they were.

I decided to pay Jack a visit. He worked on cars, and I had no idea when my little runabout had last been serviced. I didn't think I'd be biking any time soon. Not only was I pretty shaken up still, but my poor two-wheeler was banged up. I needed to get her to a bike shop and make sure she was sound before I headed out on the road again.

I decided I'd do the same for the car. Jack worked as a mechanic at Ballydehag Motors. I could take the car in and talk to Jack while he worked on her. It seemed like a brilliant plan, and so I wasted no time.

I found Ballydehag Motors without too much trouble. But from there, my plan went sadly awry when I saw the Garda vehicle parked in a visitor's bay. I pulled into the customer parking area and got out of the car.

Three car bays were open, and in the middle one, I saw Jack standing in oil-stained, blue coveralls with a hard expression on his face. In front of him were Sergeant Kelly and DI Murphy. It didn't look like a social call.

I probably should have gone back to my car and driven home, but I walked closer. Jack was facing me, and the other two had their backs to me. He glanced my way and then did a double take. The other two turned to look over their shoulders. Only Jack looked pleased to see me. Not pleased so much as desperate.

He said, "Quinn. They're arresting me for murder. But I didn't do it. Help me." There was a harsh note of appeal in his tone. I thought how this wasn't the first time he'd appealed to a woman to get him out of a jam. Sergeant Kelly finished reading him his rights and then handcuffed him and led him toward the police cruiser. DI Murphy hung back and said to me, "I'm surprised to see you here."

I gestured at my car, glad I'd come here with an excuse. "I came to get the engine looked at. It's making a funny noise."

He looked at me as though I was the one making a funny noise. "I suggest you find another mechanic."

"I thought he had an alibi for Brenda's murder?"

DI Murphy gazed toward the cruiser where his sergeant had his hand on Jack's head and was pushing him into the backseat. "It was a lie. Archie was covering up for him. After I've dealt with this idjit, I'll be back to have a word with young Archie."

Ouch. Lying to the police was never a smart idea.

And yet, I couldn't prove it, but I suspected they had arrested the wrong man.

I had a problem, though. If I wanted to save Jack, I would have to trap someone else.

CHAPTER 16

J hated what I was about to do. My only consolation was that I would see justice served. But then the police did that all day long, and at least they got paid for it. And got treated with a lot more respect than I did.

I returned to my cottage, and on the way, to my horror, the engine started making a funny noise. "And that," I said aloud, "is called being hoist with your own petard."

I managed to get the car home only to find Lochlan Balfour waiting for me outside the front door of my cottage. I knew from experience that doors and locks had no meaning to a vampire, so I appreciated the courtesy with which he'd waited outside for me. He was touching the edge of one of the beautiful, red roses that climbed all over the front of my cottage. I pulled the car up and got out, and he said, "I'm so glad the old crone didn't destroy your roses."

"Well, I think she did and then put them back again." But, like him, I was happy to see the roses looking undisturbed in spite of being surrounded and choked by thorny branches. And the scent was divine.

I unlocked the door and said, "Will you come in?"

He nodded and followed me inside. "Is there something wrong with your car? Your engine's making a funny noise."

I let out a despairing sigh. "It is. And the mechanic just got arrested."

I found it wasn't easy to surprise a vampire. Only by a fractional raising of one eyebrow did he show any surprise. "Jack, I assume."

"Yep."

He stared at my face for a slightly uncomfortable extra moment and then said, "And you don't think he killed Brenda O'Donnell."

Even more uncomfortably, he'd accurately read my thoughts. "I don't. But how to prove it?"

I explained that Archie's alibi for Jack hadn't held up. And while I didn't believe Jack had killed Brenda, I had an uncomfortable suspicion about who did.

"When I was getting a lift from Drew Milsom, he mentioned that Brenda uttered two words on the way to the hospital. The last thing she said was,"—I paused and let the drama build—"our father."

He looked as though he were waiting for more. I said, "That's it. Our father. Drew assumed that she was asking for last rites."

"And you don't think that's what she meant?"

"She seemed so modern. I felt that she was uncomfortable with the whole idea of a wake. That maybe she wasn't as traditional as her father."

"You'd be surprised how traditional people become on the brink of their deaths," Lochlan informed me. "The most hardened atheist will shout 'Help me, God' at their last."

I had an idea. Probably crazy, but something I wanted to pursue. "I'm going to do a spot of breaking and entering," I said.

"Do you want some help?"

I paused. I did and I didn't. I was hoping to rouse Biddy O'Donnell, and I wasn't certain she'd appear if a vampire was with me. I said, "I need to do the first part by myself. Can I call you later?"

"Always."

"Why are you here?" I doubted this was a social call.

"I got the results you asked for, the coroner's report."

"And?"

"Brenda O'Donnell died because of the blow from that candlestick. It had been wiped clean of fingerprints. Not much of a surprise. However, you might find some of the fingerprint results curious."

"I'm listening." More than listening, I was hanging on his every word.

He wasn't reading from a report. He'd clearly memorized it. "In the master bedroom where Brenda died, they've identified prints from Brenda, her father, you, Archie, Karen Tate, Doctor Milsom and the women who laid Billy O'Donnell out for his burial."

"Sure, that all makes sense."

"They also found prints from Jack Buckley. Because he'd been convicted of a crime, his prints were in the database."

"That's why Jack got arrested. It must be. They found the prints and focused on him."

"He's a plausible suspect. Though the evidence against him is entirely circumstantial."

I nodded. "It's almost too neat, isn't it? He supposedly

harbors a grudge against Brenda; she comes back to town, won't talk to him, so he kills her."

"It's an effective story, though, you have to admit."

"I don't know. He came to see me."

Lochlan had been relaxed. Now he stood upright and threatening. "That murderous swine came to see you? When? Where?"

"In my shop. During open hours of business."

"I don't like it. You should have called me."

I liked that my new neighbor was so protective of me, but he was going a bit far. "He wasn't threatening. He came to tell me he's in a twelve-step program and he wanted to make amends."

Lochlan made a sound of disbelief. Like coughing without opening his lips. "Easy enough to spin a tale once Brenda O'Donnell was dead. She could hardly dispute with him, could she?"

"No. But he told me he'd been to see Billy before he died. He described finding Billy in his bedroom reading a book. He said Brenda's father accepted his apology for his past behavior. If it's true, that would explain his fingerprints being in that room."

"If it's true." Lochlan did not sound convinced.

"Well, if we want to talk about spinning tales, what about Dylan? He said he was her fiancé. He said he'd only driven down that day because he'd been tied up at work, but in fact, he got fired, so he had nothing but time. Why didn't he come to her father's wake?"

"I feel certain you're going to tell me."

I was. I'd been relishing this bit of news. "Because Brenda had broken up with him."

Lochlan didn't respond dramatically, but I'd caught his interest.

"He arrived earlier than he said the day she was killed. He tried to talk to her, she blew him off. Maybe she told Archie to go for dinner so she could have it out with Dylan once and for all."

"And he killed her." He thought about that. "It's possible. But if that was true, why show up later and pretend he'd only just arrived?"

"He's a lawyer, remember. Maybe he was trying to establish his innocence. Arriving when the police were crawling all over the house. Putting on a show of grief. Rushing off to the hospital." I sighed, recalling Dylan's reaction that night. "Or his grief was genuine."

"That doesn't mean he didn't kill her," Lochlan reminded me.

I WAITED until well after dark to go to the O'Donnell place. I wore jeans and a black sweater. I didn't go as far as putting on a balaclava or darkening my face, but I kept my outfit as drab as possible, hoping to avoid notice in a town where pretty much everyone's hobby seemed to be spying on their neighbors.

I parked a block away, thinking if anyone was listening intently, the sound of my faulty engine would give me away. Still, when I got out of the car, it was quiet. Not even a dog barked. I walked as though I had every right to be on that street. Brenda's car was still parked out front, but the white van had gone. I felt a jolt of momentary anger. Had someone stolen the dead woman's stuff? Then common sense suggested it had been a rental that needed to be returned. I wondered who'd taken on that job.

Opening a locked door is not a very difficult spell, but one I've tried not to use too often. However, tonight I felt no qualms about my unauthorized entry into an empty house. I was fairly certain that both Billy O'Donnell and Brenda O'Donnell would welcome my attempts to solve Brenda's murder.

I walked in, and knowing I would meet the heaviness, I tried to welcome it. I stood still for probably two minutes, just listening. I heard nothing. Even worse, I sensed nothing.

I made a quick tour through the downstairs rooms, but everything looked exactly as it had been the night Brenda was murdered, except that the furniture and boxes had been unloaded from the rental van and brought back in. The items Brenda had intended to keep were now stacked in the front room.

With a sinking feeling, I made my way up the stairs. When the house was full of people, I hadn't noticed that the stairs creaked, but by myself, the sound of the creaking stair treads was eerily reminiscent of horror movies that had terrified me when I was young. Worse, I wouldn't be shocked to discover this was a haunted house. I already knew it. And I was dumb enough to come inside all by myself late at night.

When I got to the top of the stairs, I didn't hear movement so much as sense a presence. "Biddy O'Donnell? I need to talk to you."

There was a sound of muttering and what might have been a curse, and then, before she appeared, I smelled the body odor and old earth that I associated with her. And she came out of the master bedroom, her scraggy, old familiar following behind.

"What do you want?" They both glared at me. She sounded very suspicious, as though I was up to no good.

She was the one who was up to no good, and I knew it. "Where did you hide it?"

Those crafty old eyes were visible even in the darkness. "Where did I hide what?"

"The papers. Whatever legal papers you found that you've hidden away."

"Why would I do that?"

"To cause chaos. To buy you some time while you figure out how to make this house yours. Am I right?"

She cackled. Cackled like a crazy old witch in a cheesy horror film. "The property's mine. I already told you that."

"No. The property was yours. Hundreds of years ago. And now you are causing trouble for a lot of people." I was going to suggest to her that she might have also been partly responsible for a death, but I didn't think that would bother her. It seemed she'd been responsible for several deaths back in her time.

Self-interest drove Biddy O'Donnell. If she could be cunning, perhaps I could be cunning too. I said, "If there is no will, then a lot of very officious people will keep walking through this house. Police and lawyers and judges." I emphasized the word judges because I suspected the last time she'd met a judge, the result had been a noose around her neck. As I had hoped, she flinched at that word.

"And if I happened to see such a document? Why would I give it to you?"

"Because the more quickly we can solve the murder of the

woman who died here, the sooner I can help you secure this property for yourself."

Her gaze sharpened at that. "You'd do that?"

"I could think about it." It was a lie, but in the big picture, maybe using a lie to get at the truth was worth it.

She stared at me, and those small, black eyes narrowed. "Very well. But if this is a trick, remember, you know what I'm capable of."

"Oh yes. Are you going to wrap my cottage with tree boughs again and squeeze me to death this time?"

She looked secretly amused. "No. I have something far better in mind."

I didn't mean to be sidetracked, but I couldn't help myself. "Why did you do that? If you wanted my help? Why did you try to kill me?"

She made a sound like "pshaw." "You were never in any danger. I was merely making sure I still had the gift."

Some gift.

"Anyway, I put everything back better than I found it. The roses have an extra bloom on them now, and the dingy plaster's scrubbed up as good as new."

She was right. I thought the scent of the roses was sweeter too, but I wouldn't give her any compliments. The last thing I wanted was her meddling any more in my cottage.

Biddy O'Donnell disappeared. I didn't turn on a light because I didn't want neighbors to suspect there was someone inside. I now regretted coming so late. After a couple of nerve-stretching minutes, she returned holding a leather folder and handed it to me.

I hated going back into that bathroom where Biddy had frightened me, not once but twice. However, it was the only room I could think of that I could shut myself in and turn on the electric light without alerting nosy neighbors that there was someone in the house. There was no window in the bathroom.

So I took the leather folder into the bathroom, shut the door and turned on the light. I kept my gaze studiously away from the mirror, but I knew Biddy was there watching me. The folder contained the deed to the house and, as I had hoped, the last will and testament of Billy O'Donnell. Once again, my training in a law office came in handy, and I rapidly got to the important part of the will. And discovered I'd been right. And how I wished I hadn't been.

I said, "I need to take this away with me."

Her voice came from the mirror. "But you'll not trick me? And you'll make sure I get what I want?"

"As far as I'm able." I tapped the will in the palm of my hand. "Biddy." I wasn't sure how to phrase this. "Biddy, that skinny, red-haired woman you said you saw in this house. When was that?"

Again she looked at me rather vaguely. I had to remember that someone who had been in the ground for hundreds of years probably didn't have the most accurate sense of time. I tried again. "Was it after you frightened me in the bathroom? After you wrote that message telling me to go away?"

She nodded. "It was."

The thing with Biddy O'Donnell was, I wasn't entirely sure when to believe her. She seemed to think truth was flexible and she could bend it to suit her convenience.

Still, I had another stop to make.

I went back to my car and called Karen Tate. "I know it's

short notice and kind of late," I said. "But there's something important I need to ask you."

She seemed surprised but willing. "I live in the flat above the shop. Come around back, and I'll let you in."

My heart felt heavy as I rapped on her door. Karen looked surprised to see me on her doorstep at nine o'clock at night, but otherwise blameless. She opened the door wide and stepped back, gesturing to her clothing. "I hope you don't mind. I didn't dress for you. This is what I wear when I'm lounging around watching the telly." I completely understood, as I wore the same kinds of things in the evening. She had on soft, gray sweatpants and a striped T-shirt. Her feet were bare. "Come in."

I stepped across the threshold, feeling awful. Her eyebrows went up. "Would you like a glass of wine? Cup of tea?"

I didn't think I could accept her hospitality, not when I knew the purpose for the visit. "Would you have a glass of water?"

If my answer surprised her, she didn't show it, merely led me into the living room. It wasn't large. In fact, the whole flat wasn't very big. Still, she'd made it homey. I suspected she'd furnished the flat from her shop. It was full-on shabby chic, but charming and whimsical. "This is so pretty," I said, glancing around.

She wrinkled her nose. "I've never had any budget. My entire life, I've done everything on a shoestring."

"It's great. You have a flair."

She looked pleased and told me to sit down while she went to fetch the drinks. I didn't, though. I wandered around looking at things. In a display cabinet was a pretty tea set that I immediately recognized.

When she came back with the water, I was still standing staring at it. She said, "Ah. You've a good eye."

I turned to her then. "Even in all that junk at Billy O'Donnell's house, I noticed this tea set. It's so unusual." It was precious too. "It's Meissen, isn't it?"

She colored faintly and dropped her gaze.

She sat down and clasped her hands together. "This is an odd time for a social visit."

"It is." I didn't want to sit down. I didn't know what to do with myself. Part of me wanted to walk out again and not continue this conversation. Because I liked Karen Tate. But I had discovered that I liked truth and justice more. As pompous as that sounded, it was true.

I was trying to think how to begin when she spoke. "I don't want you to think it was stealing because it wasn't."

"Did Brenda give you that tea set?"

Now she rose too. And the two of us faced off across the compact living room. "It's complicated."

I shook my head. "No. Really, I don't think it is complicated at all." I looked at her. "Billy O'Donnell was your father."

CHAPTER 17

*H*er eyes widened, and suddenly I understood what had confused Biddy O'Donnell. Brenda O'Donnell and Karen Tate both shared their father's coloring. And they had the same build. They looked alike. Like sisters.

She let out a breath. "It's a relief to have someone finally know the truth."

"So what happened? Did you move to Ballydehag to be near your father? In the pub, you told me your father wanted nothing to do with you."

She moved over and stood at the window looking out, so all I saw was her profile. And those busy hands. Now she was playing with a silver ring, turning it around and around on her finger. "It's true. He didn't. But over time, he became more used to the idea. He wouldn't acknowledge me publicly. And that hurt a bit. No, it hurt a lot. But he used to come in my shop. Nobody thought anything of it because they knew him to be a man who loved to collect things. And we'd chat. I visited him at his house a few times. We were getting to know each other."

173

173

I nodded. "I remember when you told me about his interests. You were the only person who ever mentioned his interest in Byzantine architecture. I only knew about it because of the books."

She turned and gave a slight smile. "You're a born detective, you know."

I felt the pull of compassion, but I had to be strong. This woman wouldn't be the first to kill a sibling.

"When did Brenda find out you were her half sister?"

Any glimmer of a smile was gone now. "I was trying to tell her that day."

Not a helpful answer. "What day?"

For the first time, I saw a hint of alarm in her eyes. "The day she died. I was picking up boxes, and she looked so tired and sad, and I was tired and sad. We had a shared grief. She just didn't know it. I started to tell her, but then I stopped."

"You were worried she wouldn't take the news well?"

To my surprise, a tear rolled down her cheek. "She got a strange expression on her face, almost like she was telling me to shut up."

I didn't want to lead the witness, but I felt that she was on the brink of confessing to Brenda's murder. I stood quietly and waited.

"She was loyal to her mother, which I understood, and she'd only just lost her father. Her emotions were a mess if they were anything like mine. My timing was terrible. But she was leaving the next day. I wanted her to know." She wiped her wet cheeks. "And now she never will."

"What happened?"

She looked up in surprise. "I've just told you. That's what happened. I tried to tell her that Billy O'Donnell was my father and that we were half-sisters. I made a mess of it and gave up. And that's the last time I ever saw my sister."

"You didn't pick up a candlestick and bash her over the head?"

The blood rushed up into her face. "What?"

She looked so sincere, I almost believed her.

"You think I'd kill my own sister?"

"I think, in moments of terrible stress and pain, we sometimes do things that we later deeply regret."

"That may be true. I could imagine saying things I might regret. Maybe even throwing something. But do you really think I'd kill my flesh and blood?" She stared at me, stiff with outrage. "You have a nasty habit of accusing me of murder."

I felt puzzled. Could I be wrong? "But if you didn't kill Brenda O'Donnell, who did?"

"Are you serious? You come here from half a world away and think you understand this town and its secrets? I'd be looking at Jack Buckley, the drug dealer, myself. He's killed once. Why wouldn't he kill again?"

Since the police had Jack in custody, that seemed like the logical conclusion. But oddly, while I'd been willing to entertain Karen as a suspect, I didn't believe Jack had killed Brenda. Had I, like Brenda fallen for his cheap charm?

I drank some water. My throat felt dry. "If I've misjudged you, I'm sorry." However, I made sure not to turn my back on her.

"You've got a nerve coming here and accusing me of murder. Also, it was an idiotic thing to do. If I'd bashed one woman over the back of the head, why wouldn't I bash another?"

She was right. Though I had powers she knew nothing about. I would be harder to kill than Brenda O'Donnell.

I tried another tack. "What were you looking for when you were prowling around at the O'Donnell house?"

"What?"

"You were seen in the house after Brenda died."

"Who saw me?" She sounded belligerent, but she looked alarmed.

"A neighbor." If the word neighbor stretched to include an evil old witch who'd returned from the dead.

"I was looking for the will, if you must know." She swallowed. "My father's will."

"Why?"

"My dad, Billy O'Donnell, said he left me something in it. I wanted to take a photograph of it. So I had some evidence in case anyone tried to deny me. You may think that was small and mean of me, and perhaps it was. But whatever he'd left me was proof he cared." She swallowed. "Proof he thought of me as his daughter."

"Did you find the will?"

She shook her head. "For all I know, Brenda destroyed it."

"You haven't put any of his belongings in your shop to sell."

Her mouth twisted. "Maybe Brenda didn't want any of those things, but I did. He showed me that tea set once. It was what we used to talk about when I'd visit and, I suppose, his excuse in case anyone ever questioned him. He was showing me things that he might sell in the shop. We both shared a love of china, and so, when I saw that in the box, I thought it was something that I could always remember him by."

I said, "I'm not here to accuse you of theft. She brought

me boxes of books to sell, too, and said she didn't want any money for them. And a few of them turned out to be valuable."

She nodded. "Billy O'Donnell was a curious man. He so loved to collect things that his idea of value differed from many people's. Some things in that house were rare and valuable, but he was also interested in curiosities. Things that amused him."

I had one more question. "While you were looking for Billy O'Donnell's will, did you come across Brenda's?"

"Brenda O'Donnell's will? Why would she keep it at her dad's house? I should think it was in Dublin. Assuming she bothered to make one."

There was that. I didn't have a will. I kept thinking I should do something about it. But I didn't have any children, though I'd want Greg's daughters to have my estate. It was one of those things I kept putting off. Brenda, also a single woman about my age, could easily have been just as bad. Lawyers were notoriously terrible about taking care of their own affairs. In the same way as doctors who smoked or cobblers whose children had no shoes.

Karen seemed to give the matter some thought. "Well, if you're convinced I didn't kill my own half sister, and if Jack didn't do it, what about that flashy lawyer who showed up?"

"The flashy lawyer who showed up when?"

"The day Brenda died."

"You saw him?"

"I did. I was in my car, about to drive off, when he turned up. Brenda didn't look very pleased to see him. Maybe he killed her."

"Somebody did."

As I left Karen Tate's house, I didn't know what to think. I had already unfairly accused her of murder once. Now I'd done it again. Well, not publicly this time, at least. The trouble was, she had a really powerful motive.

She claimed she didn't know that she was in for half of Billy O'Donnell's estate, but I'd read his will. He'd split his assets between his daughters.

I didn't know a lot about Irish law, but I didn't imagine it differed greatly from American law regarding estates. If Brenda O'Donnell died without a will, then her estate would automatically go to her next of kin. And that was Karen. Had Karen Tate embraced sibling rivalry with her newfound sister? Had she killed Brenda to claim all of Billy O'Donnell's estate? I didn't want to think that. I liked Karen. We were attempting to be friends. Accusing someone of murder wasn't a brilliant way to start a friendship. She'd already been more than generous in overlooking the fact that I'd accused her once unfairly. Now I'd done it again. But, if she had killed Brenda O'Donnell, I couldn't let it go.

I found myself in a quandary.

As I walked down the quiet, darkened streets, I had another shocking thought. If I was related to Biddy O'Donnell, and all these generations later an O'Donnell was still in that house, then Karen Tate was my many times removed cousin. I'd never had cousins or family before. It was only my mother and me until she died, and then it was only me. Even if Karen Tate's cousinship was so far removed that it barely counted, it counted to me.

If only there wasn't so much suspicion in my mind directed at her.

I stopped and looked up at the sky. At the moon and the

stars and the great blackness that covered us. I had to clear my mind. That suspicion was taking up all my mental capacity. I needed to be clear and smart.

Magic is so much about focus that to remove that focus can be difficult. I breathed in and breathed out and looked at the vastness of stars and sky and took my focus from that pinpoint of light focused on Karen Tate to a broader, wider view of the universe. If I could bring that to bear on this case, then maybe I could approach it with an open mind.

When I got back to my cottage, Cerridwen was sitting in front of those beautiful roses. I'd left the outdoor light burning, and the picture could not have been prettier or more welcoming. To make it even better, she looked pleased to see me and came running forward. I scooped her up and, after pausing to literally stop and smell the roses, I let us both into the house.

"Not my finest hour, thank you for asking," I said into her soft fur. "Tonight I accused my distant cousin of murder. Not sure we'll be sharing a lot of girl time in the future."

CHAPTER 18

he next day, I decided to get a start on my project to offer books in exchange for a donation to the church restoration fund. I had so many books to get through.

I hauled two likely boxes from Billy O'Donnell's house down from upstairs. One appeared to be all about Billy O'Donnell's various collections. I thought that must be the mark of a true collector, not only to collect the thing but also to have books about the thing you collected. Here was one about toy soldiers. Another book detailed Meissen china. I put that one aside for Karen Tate, as her tea set was mentioned in the book and worth quite a sizable sum of money too.

Here was one about toy trains and a book about Marklin tin cars and trucks.

And finally a book on collecting stamps. In fact, there were several of those. Weirdly, though, for a man who collected so many things, I hadn't noticed a stamp collection.

The other box was old thrillers and romances that I

thought some older people might like. I'd leave them out for a few days, and whatever didn't sell, I would dispose of.

That done, I made a nice little sign, put out a box for donations, and took the two boxes of books outside. It was so pleasant outside that I lingered. You don't have to live in Ireland long to appreciate a sunny day when you get one. Even in summer.

In order to still look industrious, I pretended to realign the books, while really I was simply enjoying the sun on my skin. I went back inside, and then I gasped aloud and went back out again. I pulled one of the collector's books out and flipped through it. I was so engrossed in what I was doing that I didn't notice someone had come up beside me.

"Are you buying your own stock now?" an amused voice said. I glanced up to see Lochlan Balfour looking down at me. He might be a vampire, but he was one of the most gorgeous men I'd ever seen in my life.

I tried to laugh, but the sound stuck in my throat. Immediately his amusement changed to concern. "What is it?"

I glanced up and down the street as though the people of Ballydehag might suddenly all be eavesdropping at once and then gestured him inside the bookshop. Luckily, we were the only ones in there. I said, "Look at this."

I pushed the open book at him. He nodded. "I remember these. They were very popular with children before the great war. That's the First World War, I mean."

I nodded. I knew this because I'd just been reading it in the book. "Marklin tin trucks and cars are very collectible."

"I'm always surprised at the things day walkers value. They were only bits of tin meant to amuse children. Now adults who should know better buy the old faded, broken-down things, not to play with, but to display. I'm sure mankind wasn't as ridiculous when I was alive."

I raised my eyebrows. "Do the Crusades ring a bell? Subjugation of women? Their inability to own property?" I leaned closer and dropped my voice. "Witch trials?"

His lips quirked. "All right, you may have a point. Still, in all the centuries I've been around, mankind hasn't got any brighter."

I suspected he was right.

"So why are you so interested in this book? Please don't tell me you've suddenly got a passion to collect broken-down, old, tin cars?"

I shook my head. "Not me. Billy O'Donnell."

He raised his eyebrows at that. One thing about Lochlan, he had no trouble keeping up with my thought process. Which couldn't be said for everybody, sometimes including me. "And look at this," and I tapped the page I'd been staring at when he'd surprised me. "See where he's written in the values? Look at the price for that old boat."

He squinted. "Am I reading that correctly? Is that two hundred and forty thousand American dollars?"

"It is. That was the auction price. In 2011."

"So it might be worth even more now."

I wanted to slap myself upside the head. "I can't believe I've been so stupid. I remember seeing that boat shoved in a china cabinet. I think there was a tank in there as well, and a couple of cars. It struck me as such a peculiar thing to do, to put children's toys amongst china cups and teapots and a few glasses. I assumed he'd shoved any old thing in those cabinets, not having his wife around to keep the place organized."

"But now you don't think so."

"No. Now I think he kept them in the cabinet to keep the dust off them or to keep them safe. If this book proves anything, it's that he knew the value of what he owned."

"I'm not sure that's relevant anymore. They'd have gone to Brenda, but poor Brenda won't need valuable old toys now, will she?"

"No. What I'm interested in is where are those toys now?"

"They're missing?"

This was the hard part. "I don't know. Brenda boxed up so much stuff. They could be in the boxes she gave Karen Tate. They could still be in the stuff from the moving truck that got put back in the house."

He tapped his long, pale fingers on the pages of the book. He paged forward, as I had. He let out a low whistle when he saw the price of that German tank. And then the cars, real cheapies at about a hundred thousand pounds each. "There's close to a million dollars U.S. in value, according to this book and Billy O'Donnell's reckonings."

"A million dollars is a lot of money. Some people might even say it was enough to kill for."

"So what's your theory? That someone in town knew the value of what Billy O'Donnell had and stole them?"

"That's exactly what I'm thinking. And, in the middle of the theft, Brenda O'Donnell caught that person in the act."

"And so he killed her to stop her turning him in for a thief."

"Or she. What do you think? Is it much of a theory?"

"It's an excellent theory. So long as they stole the toys."

I nodded. "The first thing I have to do is go through every box and every corner of the O'Donnell house to see if they're missing."

"You'll also have to ask Karen Tate for permission to look through her boxes."

"And even then, who's to say that she didn't know that they were anything more than broken-down, old toys? She could have thrown them away." I didn't even mention the other possibility. That Karen Tate, who ran a secondhand store and had spent time with her father in his house, knew to the penny how much those toys were worth. Which only strengthened her motive to kill Brenda.

"If you want to make this theory of yours stick, Quinn, you'll have to find the stolen valuables in the hands of the thief."

He was right. There was just one enormous problem with that idea.

I had no idea who the thief was.

"Will you help me?" I asked Lochlan. I put on a whiny voice, because I couldn't bear the thought of doing all the sleuthing by myself.

"I'm happy to help. But where do we start?"

"Brenda's house. If the toys are in a moving box, then I'm wrong." I gnawed my lip. I didn't want to waste any more time. I didn't want to wait until five o'clock, when my shop closed, to start sleuthing. I had a burning sensation that I needed to get moving on this. If I had killed someone for valuable toys, I would want to get them out of my house as soon as possible. Because, if I was right, finding those toys was as good as finding a smoking gun. Or, in this case, a bloodied, heavy candlestick.

I said, "I could start right now checking the boxes at Granny's Drawers. I need to get to them before Karen unpacks them. Do you think you could watch the store for an hour?"

He glanced around as though he'd never seen the bookstore before. "You want me to be a shopkeeper?"

I rolled my eyes. "Only temporarily."

"But what do I do if someone wants to buy something?"

I thought about Kathleen and how she dealt with Danny if she needed to leave her grocery store in his charge. I said, "Tell them to write down whatever they took and the price and I'll sort it out later."

He looked a bit offended. "I'm sure I could manage a cash register, Quinn."

I gripped my lips together to stop from laughing. "Okay. Do you want a lesson?"

I could see he did. He looked as eager to play with my cash register as a little kid wanting to play store. It wasn't a very complicated machine, and he was a very smart man, so it didn't take long until he had grasped the rudiments of my cash register.

Feeling that I was leaving my store in better charge than poor Kathleen McGinnis did when she left Danny at the till, I made my way back outside and across the road and walked swiftly up to Granny's Drawers. On the way, I passed the coffee shop and, on impulse, I asked for two takeaway coffees. I thought smoothing my way with bribery would be an excellent way to get Karen's cooperation.

When I walked in, she looked amazed to see me, not surprising as we'd spent last evening together, and I'd once more practically accused her of murder. I waved the coffee at her, and she softened. Luckily, like mine, her store was currently empty of customers.

"Quinn. What a surprise." From her tone, it didn't sound like it was the greatest surprise she'd ever had.

"I need your help."

She looked even less enthusiastic. "What is it now?"

"I have an idea of who killed Brenda O'Donnell."

She didn't jump up and down with joy. "Is it me again?"

"No. Look, I'm sorry if it seemed like I was accusing you, but look at it from my point of view. You had an excellent motive." She still did, but I wouldn't get anywhere if she thought I was trying to prove she'd murdered her half sister.

"Lots of people have motives for many things they don't do. Like murder."

"Look, I can keep apologizing, or you can help me find the person who killed,"—I dropped my tone here, even though we were alone—"your sister."

"If it's illegal, I won't do it. She may have been my sister, but I don't owe her that."

"It's not illegal. All I want to do is look through the boxes you have upstairs."

That made her look puzzled. "Whatever for?"

I showed her the book. And within five minutes, I'd also shown her the pertinent pages in the book. "Did your dad ever show you those toys?"

She shrugged. "He may have. But he knew I was more interested in the china and crystal and dolls. That's what we talked about. He may have shown me a dusty old truck. He showed me all sorts of dusty, old things that I probably should have paid more attention to." Her pale skin looked blotchy, as though she'd been crying recently.

"But you weren't there to admire his collections."

She shook her head. "I wanted to be with him. I'd look at

his face to see if I could recognize myself in him. I loved his voice and tried to get him talking about the past." She laughed softly. "Like most old men, it wasn't difficult. So I might not have paid as close attention as I should have. He certainly didn't tell me about toys worth a million dollars. That I would have heard."

"Can I look through those boxes and see if I can find the toys?"

"Which would mean what? That I'd be the prime suspect again in my sister's murder?" Her voice rose a little at that.

I hastened to reassure her. "No. I don't think you killed Brenda. I also don't think those toys will turn up in those boxes. But, on the good side, if they do, you're a million dollars richer. If they don't, we have to keep looking."

She appeared to think for a moment, and I thought she might turn me down, and then she said, "I'll put the 'back in ten minutes' sign up on the door. And I'll come up and help you."

This was marvellous news. When she'd put the sign up, the pair of us went upstairs to her flat. It was unchanged from the night before. I remembered coming in here and all but accusing her of murder and felt a twinge of remorse. I would really have to get more smooth at this or, better yet, stop getting involved in murders. I had a rather blunt way of attacking people who turned out to be innocent. Especially Karen. However, she seemed to have forgiven me since she was now helping me do some sleuthing. "I keep my extra stock in the spare bedroom. It's through here."

I followed her down a narrow hall, past an old-fashioned bathroom, and she opened a closed door. I said, "Wow." It was like a treasure trove of junk. No doubt it was treasure to some, but a lot of it looked like junk to me. And there were boxes. Boxes and boxes and boxes. Boxes stacked to ceiling height, all labeled, but that was a lot of boxes. And there were bits of old furniture, a couple of cabinets, some dressmaker's dummies, an old sewing machine, a dressing table with a broken mirror. I was beginning to think she resembled her father more than she knew.

She sighed. "I know. Some of these things are lovely, they just need a little bit of loving care to bring them back. And I always think I'll have more time than I do. Anyway, I've got the boxes from the O'Donnell house here."

There were a dozen boxes. "Normally, I label everything, but I didn't get around to it."

I thought I understood. We opened the boxes. All twelve of them. Karen cried a little over a set of Royal Crown Derby teacups. She and her dad had drunk tea out of them one Sunday when she'd gone to visit him. I thought it was therapeutic for her to have someone to talk to about him, as she came to terms with her grief. There were some lovely things in the boxes, though most of it needed a good wash or dust. There was a tarnished sterling tea set that she said was Georgian, and various other beautiful things, but not a single toy, apart from three Victorian dolls with painted china faces.

As we returned everything and closed up the last box, we looked at each other. She shook her head. "Not in here."

"No." I felt simultaneously closer to discovering who had murdered Brenda O'Donnell and disappointed that, in fact, the toys hadn't turned out to be here. It was such a sordid thing to kill someone over a few old toys. Mind you, would it have been better if Karen had killed her own sister out of anger and grief and jealousy?

Murder was a thoroughly unsavory business, whatever the motive. She'd been looking sad, no doubt from going over all those things that had been her father's, and then she suddenly laughed. "You've got a smudge of dust on one cheek. And I think there's a cobweb on your elbow."

I stood up then. "I feel dusty from head to toe. I definitely need a shower."

"Well, I can offer you my bathroom, where you can wash your hands. I'll leave you to shower at your own house."

When I got back to the shop, Lochlan looked pleased with himself.

"Did you have some customers?"

"I did at that. Tourists, they were. They came in wanting a road map which I found and then I upsold them to one of your history books about County Cork."

I was delighted with him. "I'd give you a raise if I was actually paying you."

"It was my pleasure. Besides, I could tell them a bit more about the Blarney Stone and the castle than you'll find in any book."

"I don't even want to know."

"How about you? How did you make out?"

I told him that apart from getting covered in dust and grime from those boxes, I hadn't discovered a hint of the missing toys.

We agreed that our next stop was the O'Donnell home.

I thought I had one more ally in all of this. Biddy O'Donnell. Not that I wanted to talk to that dreadful old witch any more than I had to, but she'd been hanging around the O'Donnell house. I wondered if she'd seen something. I suspected I'd been asking her the wrong questions.

"Shall I come back later?" Lochlan asked.

I shook my head. I couldn't stop feeling that there was some urgency. "I'm entitled to a lunch break," I said, and put the closed sign up.

I looked at him. "Let's go catch ourselves a murderer."

"I've nothing more pressing."

CHAPTER 19

*L*ochlan said he'd drive me, and when we got outside, he unlocked a sports car. It was low, sleek and black. I felt like an international woman of mystery. I had to bend low and twist my body to get inside, but once I settled in, it was awesome. Lochlan Balfour's castle might be extremely old, but his car was anything but. We rode low to the road, and the seat hugged all my contours. "What is this?"

"A Maserati Ghibli."

I glanced at him as we pulled smoothly into the road. "Ghibli?"

"It's Arabic for hot wind."

I could see him driving at top speed, probably late at night when no one was about. However, he drove at a decorous speed to the O'Donnell home. If it weren't for the low growl of power coming from the engine, I wouldn't have known how many horses were raring to go.

We spent two hours going through every single box that Brenda had intended to take with her to Dublin and then the ones she'd left behind. If possible, it was even more heart-breaking than going through the boxes that Karen Tate had taped up in her spare room. Both spoke to the love of a daughter for her father, who was no longer there. She'd boxed up family photo albums, a book she'd won as a school prize, her christening gown. And a few treasures that I suspected reminded Brenda of her parents. An old clock, a needlework footstool.

At the end of our search, we still didn't have the toy cars.

"There's one other place I have to try," I said.

Lochlan looked at me in that pitying way people do when they know you're trying to avoid the truth. "You're going to ask Biddy O'Donnell, aren't you?"

"I am. Maybe she saw something. Maybe she has a hankering for dusty, old toys built hundreds of years after they put her in the ground." Man, that sounded weak even to my own ears.

But Lochlan Balfour didn't argue with me. He reached over and took a cobweb out of my hair. "One of the things I like best about you is your compassion."

Frankly, it was also an absolute curse. "I'll see if I can rouse Biddy. You stay here."

If he came upstairs, he would change the energy. Maybe even having him in the house would stop Biddy from appearing. So far, whenever I went in, she was happy to show herself. But with Lochlan? I wasn't certain.

I braced my shoulders as I went up those stairs once again. "Biddy?" I called out. Nothing. Echoing silence. But I knew she was there.

She wanted to play games? Fine. I stomped down the hallway. "Biddy? I know you're here."

Again nothing. Did she think she'd get rid of me that

easily? I said in a loud voice, "I'm listing the house with a real estate agent. They have this wonderful family in mind. There are thirteen children. In fact, I think the family has their own circus act. They'll be perfect companions for you. You'll hardly notice them."

Biddy O'Donnell appeared in front of me so quickly, I barely had time to stow my laugh before she was glaring at me. "What is wrong with you? Circus act?"

"Well, we could keep looking, see if we can find a quieter tenant."

Her eyes went crafty. She knew that I had deliberately lured her out. "What do you want?"

"I want to know if you saw these?" And I opened the book to the description page of the valuable toys. She put her head so close to the book, her nose nearly touched the page. Then she glanced up at me, distaste in her eyes. "What on earth would I want with this old rubbish?"

Luckily, she seemed not to have noticed the figures Billy O'Donnell had jotted in pencil. I suspected, based on what I'd heard of her, that if she did the sums in her head, she'd be very interested in those old toys.

"I don't think you'd be interested in them. I just wondered if anyone else had been in the house while you were here who'd taken them away."

She shook her head. "Not that I noticed."

"And you didn't take a liking to them yourself? You haven't tucked them away somewhere?"

She flapped her scrawny arms about like a newly hatched chick being chucked out of the nest. "I'll have you know I'm very discriminating. A bit of nasty old painted tin? No. I wouldn't want it."

She was a sly old thing, but I was sure she was telling the truth.

I wasn't sure if I was happy or sad that she didn't have the toys. "Okay. Sorry I bothered you," I said, and turned to leave.

But Biddy O'Donnell was nothing if not cunning. "Not so fast. Why? What's so important about them?"

I shrugged, trying to look nonchalant. "Sentimental value. That's all."

She sniffed. "If you've nothing more important to discuss, I have better things to do."

I couldn't imagine what those better things were, and I was way too smart to ask. I smiled. "I'll let you get on with it then."

And made my way out of there as fast as I could. I breathed deep of the fresh air when I got outside. Being around her was too much like being trapped inside a coffin with someone who hadn't bathed very often.

Lochlan was waiting outside when I came out the front door. He took one look at my face and said, "She didn't have them."

I took another deep breath of cleansing air. Shook my head. "No."

"Now what?"

"Now we track them down. Where would you sell those toys if you were trying to get your million dollars?"

Lochlan thought about it for a minute. "Dublin. It would have to be Dublin. The auctioneer might end up being in London or New York, but you'd start in Dublin."

"And we know someone who's heading back to Dublin very soon."

He nodded. "We do, at that."

It wasn't difficult to discover where Dylan McAuliffe was staying. The closest five-star hotel was Castlecork Inn, about five miles away.

"He's lost his job," Lochlan reminded me when I said I was sure we'd find him at the Castelcork Inn.

I shook my head at him. "Dylan McAuliffe may not have a job, but that won't stop him enjoying his five-star lifestyle. I'd bet on it."

Lochlan declined the bet which turned out to be an excellent decision because when I phoned Castlecork, the woman who answered said, "Yes, Dylan McAuliffe was with us for three nights, but he checked out an hour ago."

"An hour ago?"

"You just missed him," she said in a cheerful voice that had me gnashing my teeth.

"Was he headed straight back to Dublin?" I asked in the sweetest tone I could manage, considering my back molars were jammed together.

"I assume so."

I thanked her and turned to Lochlan, who'd heard the conversation. With his acute vampire hearing, he'd heard her side of it too. "Get in the car. We'll go after him."

I had a feeling this hot wind of a car would easily overtake Dylan McAuliffe's, especially as he wouldn't know we were following.

The Ghibli would definitely get us there faster than the old runabout that belonged to Lucinda and was currently making a funny noise in the engine. Maybe we were chasing a murderer, but I could enjoy the ride, couldn't I? The engine hummed, and had I not cast the odd glance at the speedometer, I would never have known how fast we were going. I said nothing to slow him down. Lochlan was an excellent driver.

He said, "Luckily, there's only one main route to Dublin."

"He's got an hour's head start. Are you sure we'll catch him?"

He glanced my way, cool and in control. "Yes."

We passed buses and trucks, what they called lorries here, wove in and out of cars, and after about two hours I said, "I think that's him, up ahead," I said, recognizing the late model BMW. There were two people in the car.

Lochlan said, "I'll wait until we're on a slightly quieter stretch of road."

I hadn't really thought this part through. "Then what will you do?"

He looked at me like I was being dim. "I'll get him to pull over."

"This isn't a movie and you're not the cops. Why would he pull over?"

"I can be very persuasive."

I didn't know if that was true or not, but sure enough, about ten minutes later, the traffic was sparse and Lochlan pulled out in front of Dylan's car, put his flicker on, slowed, and every time the car behind tried to pull around him, he'd block him.

We slowed down almost to a stop, and after a bit of honking and rude gesturing, Dylan pulled over to the side of the road.

The man who got out of the driver's side was spitting mad. "What is your problem?" he shouted. As Lochlan got out and stepped up to him, the vampire didn't speak. He just looked down from his imposing height. Something about those cold eyes seemed to have an effect, for Dylan McAuliffe took a step back and in a much less aggressive tone said, "What do you want?"

He turned to me, "Quinn?"

I was out of the car by this time. I walked up to Dylan. "I'm wondering where you're going in such a rush."

He looked puzzled but still wary. "I've seen you somewhere. Right. You were at Brenda's house the night she was killed."

"That's right. And you told me you were her fiancé."

He appeared even more wary. "So?"

"So she dumped you. Also, you said you'd left work and driven down from Dublin, but that wasn't true either, was it?"

I watched as Lochlan made his way to the passenger side. He opened the door. "Get out," was all he said.

Archie Mahoney got out of the car. He seemed much more nervous and less aggressive than the driver. He glanced at me and back at Lochlan. "Why are you here? What do you want?"

Lochlan looked into the back of the car. "What's in the backpack?"

"My clothes. What's it to do with you?"

"Archie," I said, "You didn't tell anyone you were going away. I had a few jobs for you at the bookshop."

His color had gone ruddy. "I'm only going away for a few days. Took advantage of a free ride to Dublin, didn't I?"

I took a step closer to Archie. We weren't police. We didn't have to act like them. At my nod, Lochlan opened the back door and reached in and picked up Archie's backpack. The redhead grabbed at it. "Give that back. You've got no right."

Dylan, looked torn between fury and curiosity. I said to

him, "You're my witness. I assume you're still a lawyer in good standing?"

He nodded.

Lochlan easily held the backpack out of Archie's reach while the younger man kept grabbing for it. He didn't say anything, simply passed the open pack toward me and held on to Archie. I reached inside and pulled out a green sweatshirt. I would feel terrible if my hunch was wrong. But there, under the sweatshirt, I saw a lumpy plastic bag.

I pulled it out. Archie had stopped struggling now and stood, wretched. Inside the plastic bag was the Marklin toy tank. Underneath that was the ship and then the cars, all packaged separately.

There was a moment of absolute silence, and then a truck went by, noisy and throwing up dust, and that pulled me to my senses.

"Oh, Archie," I said, so disappointed my hunch had turned out to be right. "We'll have to take you back. The Gardai will want to talk to you about these toys."

He glared at me, not looking like the sweet kid who'd hauled boxes of books so willingly. He looked angry, entitled and scared. "What about them? They're only toys. Brenda said I could have them."

I shook my head. "I don't think so."

Dylan McAuliffe spoke up. "I'm not sure what's going on. You chased him down for a few old toys? The paint's peeling off this one," he said, pointing at the ship and looking far from impressed.

"These are Marklin tin toys. Collectors' items. The total value of these is over a million dollars."

Dylan McAuliffe looked stunned and inspected the toys more carefully.

"So what?" Archie cried. "Brenda gave them to me. She did." Then he got in my face. "Prove she didn't."

"He has a fair point," Dylan the lawyer piped up. I felt like swatting him upside the head. We weren't in court, and he wasn't representing Archie.

I turned to Archie. "The police found a partial print on the candlestick that killed Brenda. It matches yours. They held off arresting you because there was no motive." I tapped the plastic bag with the tank inside it. "Here's the motive. Greed. You're going to jail, bro."

Dylan dropped the stuffy lawyer act and looked horrified. "Are you saying this ginger toad killed the woman I loved?"

"That's exactly what I'm saying."

Archie glanced up and down the road as though he might make a run for it. But he must have seen how useless that would be. He said, "I didn't. I wouldn't. These are lies."

"That partial print on the candlestick says different." I turned to Lochlan as though Archie was nothing to me. "They have all the evidence they need to convict Archie for murder." And then on a crazy bit of inspiration, I added, "I bet he murdered Billy O'Donnell too. What's the penalty for a two murders?"

Lochlan might be surprised at my leap of logic, but he hung with me. "Terrible it'd be. As young as he is, he'd never see the outside of a prison. He'd die in there."

I nodded as though I had any clue that that was true.

Luckily, Archie bought it.

"I didn't kill Billy O'Donnell. I wouldn't. I didn't mean to kill her either. She didn't know what she had. To her they were just a few dusty, old toys. But the old man, he told me all about them. Worth a fortune they were. And I needed the money. She didn't, with her fancy job in Dublin. She got out. But me? Stuck in Ballydehag for all my life? Nothing but the odd jobs man?" He shook his head. "Nobody would have missed a few tin cars, but they were my chance. Like winning the lottery."

"Brenda caught you stealing them, didn't she?" I asked softly.

He nodded, then gulped, and his Adam's apple jumped up and down. "I didn't mean to kill her. I don't know what I was thinking. She was running upstairs to call the police. Shouting at me, she was, and calling me names. I begged her not to call the Guards, but she had the phone in her hand." He put his hands over his eyes. "So I hit her with the candlestick, sitting there ready to be packed away, it was. Right there. And then she fell down and there was blood everywhere."

Dylan was staring as though stunned. A car slowed, the driver staring at us as though this were a crash site, but then seeing nothing but four people standing at the side of the road talking, sped up again.

"I wiped the candlestick clean, and I had to change my shirt. It had blood on it. I grabbed one of the old man's shirts out of the charity bag. And you were still banging on the door. I hoped you'd go away."

I nodded. "But I didn't. I came around the back and into the kitchen. And you came running down the stairs." I could still see him, red-faced and panicked. I thought he'd discovered Brenda bleeding on the floor and that explained his state, but he'd put her there. I must have arrived right after he'd done it. If only I'd been five minutes earlier, Brenda might still be alive.

Now he was confessing, he couldn't seem to stop talking. I had a feeling it was a relief to finally spill out the whole story.

"I hid the toys in a box of rubbish, then I went back the next when the police had finished to fetch them." He rubbed his face. "I'm sorry. I didn't mean this to happen."

Dylan McAuliffe had worked himself up into a mighty passion, and before I saw the blow headed for Archie's head, Lochlan had stepped in and grabbed his fist.

"Let's let the law deal with him," he said in his cold way.

"But Brenda was going to be my wife. And he killed her."

I shook my head. "She was never going to be your wife. And you knew that. She'd already broken up with you. What were you even doing there?"

To my shock, his eyes filled with tears. "I was hoping to get her back. I had nothing left. I lost my job. I'd lost Brenda. I thought, maybe if I could get her back, then everything would go back to normal."

He had no idea how close he'd come to being tried for murder.

He glared at Archie. "And you! I thought you were a nice kid. Drove me to the hospital to see Brenda. You were so friendly. Helped take my mind off it. You only did drove me so you could see if she'd made it. See if she'd told the Guards what you did."

"No."

"I'm not taking you one more kilometer in my car." He pointed his index finger at the killer. "I don't ever want to see you again."

That was a slight problem because Lochlan's fancy car only had room for two. I said, "I'd better call the Gardaí. But please wait until they get here so you can confirm that you heard Archie admit to murder."

He nodded jerkily. "For Brenda's sake."

He looked at the bags of toys glinting in the sun and then shook his head. "You killed a woman for a few dusty old toys."

CHAPTER 20

"$\mathcal{D}$id they really find a partial print on that candlestick?" Deirdre asked. We were supposedly having a meeting of the vampire book club, but nobody had even bothered to bring the book.

I shook my head. "I was totally bluffing. I knew that if he stuck to his story that Brenda had given him those toys, we couldn't prove he'd killed her. I had to get a confession out of him." Lochlan had seen the forensics report and knew I was bluffing, but he'd played along.

"And that was genius that you turned on your cellphone to record," she said to Lochlan.

"That was only insurance. Quinn had the brilliant idea of making Dylan McAuliffe a witness. He'll have more credibility, being a solicitor. Even if he was unemployed."

"Dylan's hoping to get a job in the prosecutor's office," I said. "I think being involved in a murder case lit a fire in his belly."

"Archie Mahoney confessed to the Gardaí. They have his sworn, signed confession," Lochlan said.

"And Jack Buckley's a free man."

Lady Cork looked from Lochlan to me. "You two make a wonderful detective team."

~

A WEEK after Archie's arrest, Karen Tate and I met for dinner at the pub. I had a feeling this might become a regular event, one I would more and more look forward to. Especially if I could stop accusing my distant cousin of murder.

This time, I was the first one there. I said hello to Sean O'Grady and asked for a bottle of red wine and two glasses. Then I said, "No, make that champagne. The proper French stuff."

He looked very impressed. "We don't get much call for fancy fizz around these parts."

I put on a shocked face. "Don't tell me you don't stock French champagne in your cellar."

"Keep your knickers on. Course I stock champagne. Just don't get much cause to serve it. Is there a special occasion?"

I nodded. "There is. But I'm not at liberty to tell you what."

"A mysterious American. You don't see that every day." He grinned to take the sting out of his teasing words.

I leaned across the bar and punched him lightly on the shoulder. "Just get me that champagne."

So when Karen arrived, not only was I already there at the same table we'd sat at before, but there was a silver ice bucket of cooling champagne, and Sean had brought over proper champagne flutes.

She sat down and said, "Sorry I'm late. I was with the lawyers."

"And?"

She looked torn between happy and sad. "And you were right. Brenda never made a will."

"So if she died intestate, I'm guessing you were her next of kin."

She nodded. "I was. And since our father left each of us half of his estate, her half comes to me."

"She'd want that. In fact, they'd both want that," I assured her.

I couldn't open the champagne yet. I felt her conflicted emotions too clearly.

"What if she hated me? I mean, what if she would have hated me if she'd known?"

I told her something I had figured out only recently. "She did know you were her sister."

Karen shook her head. "That's not true. I wanted to tell her, but I couldn't."

"It is." I leaned closer. "Dr. Milsom told me she spoke two words before she died. They were, 'our father.'"

She glanced up, and our gazes held. "Our father? Maybe she wanted him to say the Lord's Prayer."

I nodded. "He thought she was asking for last rites. But I think she was trying to tell him you were her sister and Billy had acknowledged you. She had so little strength, all she could manage was 'our father.' Remember, he hung on after he had his heart attack. He hung on until she got there and could speak to her."

"You think that's what he wanted to say?"

"Among other things. I do."

She looked so much happier. She blinked back tears. "I think Brenda and I would have been friends if she'd lived."

"I think so too." I paused. "But because of Archie thinking he could grab those toys and her walking in right at the wrong moment, you'll never get the chance."

She blinked rapidly again. "I'd have given them to him. If it meant I could have kept my sister. What were a few old tin toys to me?"

"I know. If we could turn back time." How many different decisions would any of us make if we had that luxury.

"Well, I've made one decision."

"What's that?"

"I'm donating those toys to Father O'Flanagan to help with the restoration of the church tower and the graveyard." She shook her head. "I could never live with myself if I used that money for something selfish, when those toys caused my sister's murder. Brenda's buried with our dad and her mum in the graveyard. It seemed the right thing to do."

I leaned closer, "That's a wonderful idea. And, if it's okay with you, I'll do the same thing with the first edition of the Winnie-the-Pooh and the signed Ian Fleming that Brenda put in a box for me to sell at my shop."

Her eyes lit up. "Between us, we may raise enough to fix that old church steeple and the graveyard."

Now I felt that we could celebrate. I pulled the champagne out of the bucket. Sean O'Grady had been keeping half an eye on us, and he rushed forward.

"Ladies, allow me."

Naturally, we let him. He opened the champagne with the perfect amount of pop and then poured the bubbling wine into our glasses.

Karen lifted her glass. "I want to make a toast."

"Okay."

She thought for a minute and then said, "To Brenda and Billy. To family. And new friends." She clinked my glass, and we sipped.

Karen leaned back in her seat. "I think you were the first person who said what a wonderful bed-and-breakfast that old house would make. That's what I'm going to do with the O'Donnell house. What do you think?"

When I'd said the O'Donnell house would be a great B&B, I hadn't realized that a nasty, old witch had taken to living there. "Are you sure? Running a bed-and-breakfast is a lot of work."

She nodded. "I am sure. I've thought of nothing else. Naturally, I can furnish the entire place with the things in my shop, and the furniture that was already there. It will take some money, but I've already talked to the bank about a loan."

I didn't know what to say, so I went with, "I heard the house was haunted."

Her eyes shone. "Oh, I hope so. Nothing will bring in the tourists like ghost stories."

I had to laugh. Biddy O'Donnell would have a fit if she found herself a tourist attraction. I couldn't think of anything better. We both sipped champagne.

"I'm sorry I didn't get a sister, but I feel like I've made a fast friend."

I was flattered and told her I felt the same way.

Then a voice interrupted our BFF bonding. "What's the occasion?" Andrew Milsom asked.

Karen looked at me, and there was a spark of competition

in her gaze. So much for the sisterly bonding. She said, "I'm opening a bed-and-breakfast in the O'Donnell place."

He looked very impressed. "Are you now? That is something to celebrate."

She said, "Get Sean to give you a glass, and I'll pour you some champagne."

"Champagne's not my usual drink, but don't mind if I do."

Soon the three of us were sipping champagne. I thought, since I had already accused Karen Tate twice of being a murderer, I really owed her one. So I finished my second glass of champagne and then said, "I'm almost positive I forgot to lock up my shop. I'm so sorry. I have to leave you now."

Andrew Milsom looked surprised, but Karen knew exactly what I was doing. She said, "I'll call you tomorrow."

I knew she would. I wondered what she'd have to report.

I headed out into the soft summer evening. "Good evening, Quinn," said Kate O'Leary and her husband as they headed into the pub.

"Evening." I loved that people here were beginning to know me and I them.

I got on my newly fixed bicycle and headed back to my cottage. I'd been looking forward to my pub dinner, but I thought a nice evening with my familiar and a dinner I'd take out of the freezer wasn't a terrible idea.

I'd had worse Friday nights.

I pedaled up the gravel drive, got off my bicycle and leaned it against the potting shed under the overhanging roof. I took off my brand new bike helmet and took it into the shed. It was warm in there and smelled of drying herbs. On impulse, I checked the yew branch I'd brought in here to dry.

At least if Biddy decided to wrap the place in yew again, hopefully the spell would only affect the shed.

The yew was drying nicely, and my palm and fingers tingles as I touched the wood. I knew that Pendress and the other witches would do everything they could to return Biddy to her subterranean prison. I was certain the old witch wasn't going back there without a fight. With her blood in my veins and a wand from this powerful magic tree, I had an idea I might be able to stop Biddy from doing anything too terrible. Maybe my compassion was getting the better of me again, but I would not let them put her her back in the ground. However, I wasn't going to let her terrorize Ballydehag, either.

I left the potting shed and let myself into my cottage. Cerridwen padded out to rub against my legs meowing. I wanted to believe it was purely love making her so affectionate, but it was also dinner time. I opened a can of her favorite cat food, then I opened the fridge to see what I could find for myself.

Cream, some mushrooms that wouldn't last much longer. I opened the freezer and saw I had some frozen lobster meat. Then I remembered why. Kathleen had raved about a recipe called Dublin Lawyer. "Ever so easy, it is," she'd promised me as she sold me the ingredients. Lobster, cream, Irish whiskey, mushrooms, scallions and spices. Served over rice. I decided making Dublin Lawyer was a perfect tribute to Brenda. I'd have my own private wake.

I followed the recipe Kathleen had given me. Cerridwen happily gobbled a chunk of lobster I popped in her dish.

When my meal was ready, I took it into the front room. I opened the windows to let in the ocean breeze. I lit candles and settled in my favorite chair. I even had a small glass of whiskey, which Kathleen had told me was the correct drink to go with Dublin Lawyer.

I lifted my glass in a toast. "Brenda, I didn't know you well, but I think we could have been friends. I believe Dylan will make sure your killer is properly dealt with. I'll look out for your sister, and your old home. Godspeed." And then I sipped the whiskey.

The Dublin Lawyer was rich and delicious and perfect with a glass of whiskey.

When I'd finished dinner, I got out the book we'd be reading for the next meeting of the vampire book club. Cerridwen jumped into my lap and curled up. If I looked out the window and to the west, I could see Devil's Keep standing dark and tall and oddly comforting now I knew the occupants.

I heard the soft murmuring of the waves as I opened the book and read aloud, in case Cerridwen was in a bookish mood. "Call me Ishmael. Some years ago—never mind how long precisely—having little or no money in my purse, and nothing particular to interest me on shore, I thought I would sail about a little and see the watery part of the world."

I glanced up at this watery part of the world. I'd come ashore in Ballydehag, County Cork, thinking it would be a quiet, dull life. I could not have been more wrong. I wondered what fresh adventures waited. In the meantime, I went back to Moby Dick.

~

Thanks reading for *Chapter and Curse!* I hope you enjoyed

Quinn's adventure. Keep reading for a sneak peek of the next mystery, *A Spelling Mistake*, Vampire Book Club Book 3.

A Spelling Mistake, Chapter 1

VAMPIRES AREN'T the most excitable of creatures. At least not usually. However, when the vampire book club met that Tuesday night, I felt waves of nervous energy coming from Bartholomew Branson.

Bartholomew was the most recent member of the club, having only been turned a few months earlier. A world-famous thriller writer, Bartholomew had taken part in a cruise where his fans had adored him so much that he ended up getting drunk and attempting to re-enact a dangerous stunt from one of his books.

The result would have been a watery grave off the coast of Ireland except that one of his fans was undead and, unable to see the author perish, turned him into a vampire. He was too well known to appear in public in a big city and had somehow ended up here, in the small town of Ballydehag, in County Cork where a quaint bookshop called The Blarney Tome was run by a witch. That would be me.

Bartholomew was not happy. He wasn't a literary giant, and his thrillers would probably not stand the test of time, but he'd loved the limelight and lifestyle of celebrity. Now, that life was over and he was forced to remain out of sight and keep a very low profile. Even more painful, his final book was being released posthumously.

"I love launch parties," he said, "The champagne, the book sales, the long line of fans waiting for autographs."

"The fleeting nature of fame," Oscar Wilde put in. Oscar had proven that his literary genius was as immortal as he was, and he never wasted an opportunity to put Bartholomew in his place. Far, far down the hierarchy of literature.

"I had so many books I still planned to write. My career was really taking off," Bartholomew wailed.

"Ambition is the last refuge of the failure," Oscar said, picking a piece of lint from his purple velvet suit.

Bartholomew rose and turned to Oscar, his hands fisting. "Look here, you Irish windbag, I may not write literature nobody ever reads, but my fans love me. All I want is one final launch party. Is that too much to ask?"

I felt so bad for him. I glanced at Lochlan Balfour, who ran the vampire book club. I sensed he was sympathetic, but no one could give Bartholomew Branson what he'd lost.

I did have something I could offer and now seemed a good time to reveal it. "I have a surprise for you," I told the wretched thriller writer. "I've ordered two dozen hardcover copies of your new thriller. I'll feature them in the front window of the store, but we'll also read your book as our next book club selection." Bartholomew was always nominating his own books for the club and consistently rejected.

"Pass me my smelling salts," Oscar moaned. "I'm about to faint with horror."

But Bartholomew didn't even hear the latest insult. He rushed up to me, picked me up off my feet and swung me in a circle. "That's a great idea," he said. "We'll have my final book launch, right here." Then he put me down and stepped back. "Wait. I've got an even better idea. We'll do the real launch here. Don't worry, Quinn. I'll take care of everything. You sign the letters I dictate. I know exactly how to get the Irish launch here." He chuckled and rubbed his hands together. "Oh, don't look so shocked. I know I can't be at the party, but I can watch. That's almost as good as being there. Quinn, this event will put your little bookshop on the map."

How had a small favor to make Bartholomew feel better turned into this truly terrible plan?

And how would I stop him?

Order your copy today! *A Spelling Mistake* is Book 3 in the Vampire Book Club series.

A Note from Nancy

Dear Reader,

Thank you for reading *Chapter and Curse*. It was such a joy to write. I hope you'll consider leaving a review and please tell your friends who like paranormal women's fiction and cozy mysteries. Review on Amazon, Goodreads or BookBub.

If you enjoy paranormal cozy mysteries, you might also enjoy the *Vampire Knitting Club* - a story that NYT Bestselling Author Jenn McKinlay calls "a delightful paranormal cozy mystery perfectly set in a knitting shop in Oxford, England. With intrepid, late blooming amateur sleuth, Lucy Swift, and a cast of truly unforgettable characters, this mystery delivers all the goods."

Join my newsletter for a free prequel, *Tangles and Treasons*, the exciting tale of how the gorgeous Rafe Crosyer, from The Vampire Knitting Club series, was turned into a vampire.

I hope to see you in my private Facebook Group. It's a lot of fun. www.facebook.com/groups/NancyWarrenKnitwits

Until next time,
Happy Reading,

Nancy

Vampire Book Club: Paranormal Women's Fiction Cozy Mystery

Crossing the Lines - Prequel

The Vampire Book Club - Book 1

Chapter and Curse - Book 2

A Spelling Mistake - Book 3

A Poisonous Review - Book 4

Village Flower Shop: Paranormal Cozy Mystery

Peony Dreadful - Book 1

Vampire Knitting Club: Paranormal Cozy Mystery

Tangles and Treasons - a free prequel for Nancy's newsletter
subscribers

The Vampire Knitting Club - Book 1

Stitches and Witches - Book 2

Crochet and Cauldrons - Book 3

The Great Witches Baking Show: Culinary Cozy Mystery

Gingerdead House - A Holiday Whodunnit

The Great Witches Baking Show Boxed Set: Books 1-3

Abigail Dixon: A 1920s Cozy Historical Mystery

In 1920s Paris everything is très chic, except murder.

Death of a Flapper - Book 1

Toni Diamond Mysteries

Toni is a successful saleswoman for Lady Bianca Cosmetics in this series of humorous cozy mysteries.

Frosted Shadow - Book 1

Ultimate Concealer - Book 2

Midnight Shimmer - Book 3

A Diamond Choker For Christmas - A Holiday Whodunnit

Toni Diamond Mysteries Boxed Set: Books 1-4

The Almost Wives Club

An enchanted wedding dress is a matchmaker in this series of romantic comedies where five runaway brides find out who the best men really are!

The Almost Wives Club: Kate - Book 1

Secondhand Bride - Book 2

Bridesmaid for Hire - Book 3

The Wedding Flight - Book 4

If the Dress Fits - Book 5

The Almost Wives Club Boxed Set: Books 1-5

Take a Chance series

Meet the Chance family, a cobbled together family of eleven kids who are all grown up and finding their ways in life and love.

Chance Encounter - Prequel

Kiss a Girl in the Rain - Book 1

Iris in Bloom - Book 2

Blueprint for a Kiss - Book 3

Every Rose - Book 4

Love to Go - Book 5

The Sheriff's Sweet Surrender - Book 6

The Daisy Game - Book 7

Take a Chance Boxed Set: Prequel and Books 1-3

For a complete list of books, check out Nancy's website at NancyWarrenAuthor.com

ABOUT THE AUTHOR

Nancy Warren is the USA Today Bestselling author of more than 100 novels. She's originally from Vancouver, Canada, though she tends to wander and has lived in England, Italy and California at various times. While living in Oxford she dreamed up The Vampire Knitting Club. Favorite moments include being the answer to a crossword puzzle clue in Canada's National Post newspaper, being featured on the front page of the New York Times when her book Speed Dating launched Harlequin's NASCAR series, and being nominated three times for Romance Writers of America's RITA award. She has an MA in Creative Writing from Bath Spa University. She's an avid hiker, loves chocolate and most of all, loves to hear from readers!

The best way to stay in touch is to sign up for Nancy's newsletter at NancyWarrenAuthor.com or join her private Facebook group facebook.com/groups/NancyWarrenKnitwits

To learn more about Nancy and her books
NancyWarrenAuthor.com

facebook.com/AuthorNancyWarren

twitter.com/nancywarren1

instagram.com/nancywarrenauthor

amazon.com/Nancy-Warren/e/B001H6NM5Q

goodreads.com/nancywarren

bookbub.com/authors/nancy-warren

Printed in Great Britain
by Amazon

79003426R00132